A HIP-HOP LOVE IN HOLLYWOOD

A Rap Fairytale

BARBIE SCOTT

Shan Presents, LLC

A Hip-Hop Love in Hollywood

Copyright © 2019 by Barbie Scott

Published by Shan Presents

www.shanpresents.com

Subscribe

Text Shan to 22828 to stay up to date with new releases, sneak peeks, contest, and more....

Submissions

To submit your manuscript to Shan Presents, please send
the first three chapters and synopsis to
submissions@shanpresents.com

Prologue
BLAKE BAILEE

"*Amazing grace*
How sweet the sound
That saved a wretch like me
I once was lost, but now I'm found
Was blind, but now I see"

AS THE CROWD *began to clap tears poured from my eyes. I don't know what it was about this song that always made me so emotional. When I looked out into the crowd I wasn't the only one crying. My aunt Ellie had tears running down her face and a few elder ladies amongst the audience as well. As we walked off the stage, Pastor Reese stepped around into his pulpit and began reading a scripture from his bible. I sat in the stands along with the rest of the choir and bowed my head for the last prayer. After, aunt Ellie and I were gonna go grab something to eat from Hometown Buffet just as we'd done every Sunday. It was either Hometown or Sizzler which was one of my favorites. I couldn't wait because I was starving.*

. . .

JUST AS OUR service was over, everyone told me how great I had done during my solo. Smiling hard I took pride in my voice because no lie I could really sing. Although the choir wasn't where I attentively wanted to express my vocals I was only fifteen so this would have to do. Often I had dreams of becoming a famous singer and I spent most of my days locked away in my room holding my own concerts. I would dress up in my mother's worn down heels, grab the broom stick and pretend I was in the middle of the Staple Center for a sold out show. I did this every day and each day I felt closer to stardom. Well that's until my mother would break me from my adoring dream with all her yelling and screaming.

"Bitch you can't sing so shut the fuck up!" her voice would echo throughout our empty apartment. I swear I couldn't stand her ass.

"Blake baby, we have to go." aunt Ellie rushed over to me bringing me from my daze. "I have to catch my flight at 2." I looked at her not understanding what she meant.

"Aunt E, we not going to Hometown?"

"No baby. Aunty is leaving to Texas."

"Texas, for how long?" I asked just as we got to her car. Before she answered she climbed inside and reached over to unlock my door. She started her engine and drove away from our church. "How long?" I asked again. Before she replied, she let out a soft sigh.

"I'm moving baby." she said and my chest instantly got tight. Aunt Ellie was all I had so hearing this news didn't sit well with me.

"So when was you gonna tell me his?"

"I'm sorry Blake. It's just, uhhh, I really didn't know how to tell you. Everything in California is so damn expensive I can't afford to live here. My grandfather is gonna rent his home to me but you can come visit whenever you want." she continued to give me her sob story but I tuned her ass out.

"AMAZING GRACE
How sweet the sound

That saved a wretch like me
I once was lost, but now I'm found
Was blind, but now I see"

I KNEW it was disrespectful but right now I didn't care. I began singing with my fingers plunged into my ears so I couldn't hear another word from her. From the side of my eye I could see aunt Ellie shaking her head but I really didn't care. She could shake it all she wanted because the fact still remains, she was leaving and wasn't taking me with her. Right now, I hated aunt Ellie just as much as I hated my mother, so when I noticed we were at my home I jumped from her car and slammed the door without even saying goodbye. I ran full speed to my mother's front door and it was open. I slammed the door and locked it behind me but instead of running to my room I turned to see if my aunt would come back for me. I just knew she would. Aunt E, loved me, so she wouldn't dare leave me; or so I thought. Instead, her car pulled off from alongside the curb and I watched it until the tail end had disappeared up the street. Letting out a deep sigh my body felt drained and all I wanted to do was lay down.

"IS THIS THE ONE?" I turned around to the voice and when I noticed a man by the name of Lenox sitting in my living room my heart began to pump. Lenox had a bad reputation in my neighborhood so him being in my home told me it was trouble.

"Yeah that's her. Take her ass and gone Lenox." my mother replied smacking her lips like she always done. You know that crack-head smack like they always had a jawbreaker candy in their mouth? She and all her friends had that same smack and of course all her friends were crackheads.

"Take me where?" I asked with my face twisted.

"Don't ask no muthafucking questions Blake. Just go pack all yo shit and go!" she shouted making me nearly jump out of my skin. I

scurried off into my bedroom and began throwing my clothes into a bag. I don't know where the hell I was going but if it meant getting away from this hell-hole then so be it. I really hated my mother and the way she was raising me and this is why my heart was crushed with aunt Ellie. She knew how much I hated it here which is why she made it her business to rescue me nearly every day. Because aunt Ellie didn't have any kids she treated me as her own and even bought me things that my mother never bought me.

LINDA BAILEE WAS FAR from a mother. The only thing she did do for me was buy me old clothes from the thrift store with the county check she received monthly. She barely fed me and when she did it was always spaghetti or noodles. I don't know why but she hated my guts. I didn't understand why because I loved her raggedy ass to death. No matter how many times she had beat me until I passed out, or how much she verbally attacked me, she was still my mother.

"HURRY YO ASS UP BLAKE; we ain't got all day!" I heard her scream from the kitchen. Slamming the remainder of my items into a bag, I headed out of my room before she came in swinging. Just as I made it to the area her and Lenox sat, I noticed him slide her a clear baggie full of white substance. Her eyes lit up wide as she watched the bag in front of her. She quickly snatched it off the table and jumped to her feet. Lenox stood to his feet and when our eyes locked, it was something about the way he looked at me that made my insides cringe. I was still unsure of what was going on and when Lenox waltzed over to the door he looked back and motioned for me to come. For a brief moment I stood frozen until my mother began to scream.

"Gone little bitch!"

Yung Baby

"ARE YOU ON YOUR WAY?"

"Man, I said I needed to handle some shit and I was coming."

"Well, you need to hurry up, Baby; her fever is 104."

"Aight man. I'm on my way."

I busted a U-turn and headed for my baby moms' crib. She knew when it came to my daughter I'd drop everything I was doing. Emani was a nigga world. Although having her with Tristian was an accident, I would never regret my daughter.

Tristian and I met one night after one of my shows in NY. When I say she was bad, hands down, she was the baddest bitch in the room that night. After taking her back to my hotel, we smashed and it was something about her that made me keep in contact, so if I wasn't in her city, then I was flying her in.

At first, Tristian was cool as fuck. When she came to our hotels, she never tripped on the many women we kept around us. That's until, her ass got pregnant and turned into the baby mama from hell. She wasn't as bad as most bitches, but she used the baby to get her way. She moved down to Cali, so I could be near Mani and that's when all hell broke loose. Tristian wanted to be more than just my baby mama, and if she didn't do all the fuck shit she was doing, I may have given her a ring. Her last straw was when she hopped on social and lied to the world about me giving her a disease. That shit went viral so fast, but I had something for her stupid ass.

I sued her ass for Defamation of Character. I wasn't gonna actually take her money because truth be told, she ain't have shit. Everything she had was mines, but I wanted her to see how it felt to be humiliated by the world. She caught so much backlash from my fans, she deactivated her Instagram and barely went outside. Since then, I really hadn't had any problems out of her except her begging to be a family. Hell no, wasn't happening. I was loving being single and the

5

way my career was going, there was too many fish in the sea for a shark like me.

JUST AS *I made my illegal U-turn, I noticed flashing lights behind me. In my rear view, I could see the blue and red lights, so I pulled over to the side of the curb. "Shit," I cursed myself because one thing about the LAPD, they didn't care if you had the proper documentation; they would still search yo shit.*

"Step out of the car!" one officer approached my window.

"Step out the car? The fuck you mean. I got license and insurance sir, and I'm not on probation or parole so no I ain't stepping out."

"Woo, that's Yung Baby." another officer boasted as he looked inside my whip. The first officer looked at him then looked at me, but he wasn't moved by my celebrity status.

"Step out of the car!" again he shouted. I shook my head because I knew exactly where this shit was going. Letting out a sigh, I thought about the 9 mm I had under my seat. The weed wasn't shit because marijuana is now legal in my town. I also knew if I tried to reach for my strap they would probably pop my ass, so I was in a lose-lose situation.

"Open the door nice and slow." he said with the flashlight nearly blinding me. When I opened my door and stepped out, one officer grabbed me and pulled me over to the sidewalk. The asshole officer began searching my whip and when he flashed his light underneath my driver seat my heart fell into my stomach.

"We got a gun!" he yelled out making the other officer look my way. I shook my head because I knew after this they were taking my black ass in. Before I knew it, four more cars had pulled up, and they had me standing out here for over an hour while they continued to search.

CALIFORNIA - U.S. RAPPER Yung Baby pleaded guilty on Thursday for criminal possession of a weapon in a June 19th incident and will serve 2 years in prison, Los Angeles City prosecutors said.

Yung Baby, 24, who won best rap album at the 2018 Grammy Awards and whose real name is Baby Damone Taylor, agreed to a plea deal with prosecutors and will be sentenced at Superior Court of California in September.

After spending a few months out on bail, I decided to take the deal for 2 years. I wasn't about to go to trial and play with them racist muthafuckas. My max was ten years and it would be just my luck they hit a nigga with nearly that. I had 2 weeks until my court date and the only thing I looked forward to was seeing my daughter. Tristian promised to bring her to court because she hadn't brought her once to see me. She mentioned how dirty the county was, and she promised when I hit the pen she would come.

I had already made arrangements with ma dukes to bring Emani up there because I didn't need Tristian getting the wrong ideas. I knew if she came to visit she would think we were a couple and that wasn't happening. I didn't need her to hold me down because a nigga was well-paid. Keep shit real, I was mentally prepared to serve this little time and come back home to my fans.

1

Mic Check 1

BLAKE 'PURE SEDUCTION' BAILEE

---

3 years Later...

"SO YOUR BIG day is coming. You excited Blake?"

"Hell yeah, I can't wait to get out of here. I've given these people enough of my time."

"I know. Now that you're eighteen you gotta be careful. You were lucky to come to juvie because I hear lots of crazy stories about the big house." Meeah said referring to the adult women's prison. "So what you gonna do when you get out? You can't go back out there. Next time won't be so peachy."

"I know. I'm done with that shit Meeah." I let out a frustrated sigh. I had given these people two long years and I refused to come back.

"But what you gone do about Lenox because from the stories you tell, he's not letting up."

"I really don't know. He's gonna have to understand." I replied as I continued packing my belongings. All my hygiene and food I was leaving with Meeah, so all I pretty much had were the clothes Lenox sent in my packages and letters and cards from Courtney.

"Well good luck." Meeah began fluffing her pillow so she could lay down. I began to do the same then laid back on my bunk and fell into a daze. I had less than a week to be released and a part of me was nervous. It had been two years out of my four year sentencing and because I didn't have a plan I was confounded. I was sentenced to four years with half time because this was my third charge for prostitution. Every day I spent locked away I missed my freedom more. I mean my life wasn't shit but on the streets I only had to answer to one person. *Lenox*. In here, I had guards constantly telling me what to do, yelling for no damn reason and treating us like animals. I was locked up for making money not murder but that's how they treated me.

LENOX, who my mother had basically sold me to, had been here to hold me down the entire ride. The day I left my mother's home, he took me in and what I considered a good deed turned out to be a project. Well that's what Lenox referred to me as; his damn project. He told me he had been watching me for years and couldn't wait to get his hands on me. I thought he had meant sex, and I was scared to death. To my surprise, he moved me into his home and had not touched me. He moved me in, along with three other girls and my naive ass thought they were really his sisters. That's until one night, I walked in on him and two others, and they were all naked sprawled out in his bed. One, who name was Champagne, was sucking his dick while the other fondled her.

Out of all the girls, I met one who I really liked and her name was Courtney. Which is the one who would always write and come visit. I was the youngest amongst us all, so they nicknamed me *Pure*. Whatever that meant. I guess I couldn't complain because it was a major change from my mother. However, three months later, my hair was done up, and I was wearing a dress that made me appear older than fifteen. Lenox, along with the girls, took me to a party and imagine my surprise when I thought we were there for fun. Before I knew it, I was forced into a room with a Caucasian man and Lenox demanded I had sex with him. The entire time I cried and Lenox threatened to send me back to my mother. A part of me wanted to go, but this living situation seemed about the same; pure fucking torture. The only difference was, Lenox and the girls loved me like family. Or at least that's what I was trained to believe.

Before I knew it, I had become Lenox's bottom bitch and had sucked more dicks than Blow Pops. I sold myself for *the family* as he called it and I did this for an entire year. I was arrested twice and I guess the judge was tired of my ass because he sentenced me to four years with half time. To my surprise, Lenox held me down while in jail and even had the girls visit me. No matter how many times I told him I didn't wanna go back to those streets, his reply was always "we'll figure something out," so here I was, ready to be let free and I didn't know what the future had for me. I mentioned getting a job a few times and each time he would brush it off with "my girls don't work"… another dumb reply that I would always have to brush under the rug.

$$$

"WELCOME HOME!" Courtney smiled as I climbed into the car. After replying, thank you, I looked back to the facility and although I was happy to be out, I knew I was gonna miss Meeah. Over the course of time, Meeah and I had become really close. She was the only one I dealt with in jail and I promised to come visit. She was serving time for assault on a peace officer, attempt to commit robbery and assault with a deadly weapon. She had already been locked up three years but she had another year left on her sentencing.

"Lenox and the girls are waiting for you. He sent Ernestine to go shopping for you and Champagne gonna hook your hair up." I nodded my head without replying because I was too nervous to ask what was the special occasion.

"Don't look like that Blake. I don't think you going back on the streets." Courtney said making me sigh in relief.

"I hope not. I'm done with that shit."

"Let's just hope he doesn't put you on Back Page because that's where me and Ernestine been working off of. Other than that, we've moved to Hollywood and Sunset Blvd is where all the money is."

"What's Champagne been doing?"

"That bitch." Courtney rolled her eyes. She couldn't stand Champagne and I couldn't blame her. She was a real *Lenox kiss ass* and the bitch couldn't stand none of us. She wanted Lenox to herself and no matter how many times he beat her ass, she was infatuated with him. "She's working down at Crazy Girlz."

"She dancing?"

"Yeah and that bitch be racking up bread too. I mean she doesn't make as much as us because of course Daddy got us working on rich, White men, but she stacking enough to keep him happy."

"Oh." was all I replied. The car fell silent and before I knew it, we were pulling up to the 5 bedroom home located in the heart of Hollywood.

WHEN I EXITED the vehicle I made my way up the few stairs and headed inside. The house seemed pretty quiet and it didn't surprise me because everyone was always working.

"Daddy wants you." Champagne appeared from nowhere and spoke with her usual eye roll. Instead of responding, I headed for his room and pushed open the door. Lenox sat in his usual spot which was on a plush white two seater sofa that matched his room decor. He had on a silk robe and was puffing on a cigar. I wanted so bad to laugh because this nigga was always so animated. He watched too many damn movies and Scarface was one.

"Welcome home Pure." he smiled taking a toke from his cigar.

"Hey Daddyyy." I walked over to give him a hug.

"Now that your home, we gotta get you back to work. Yo fine ass been making Daddy miss money. Tonight I'm gonna let you relax but tomorrow, it's back to work."

"But Daddy I don't wanna go back on the streets." I whined.

"You're not. I hollered at a buddy of mine, and he gone give you a shot at Crazy Girlz. Now I know you know how to dance so you'll do well on stage. Shit pays good too. We also have a private room set up upstairs so you don't have to walk the blade anymore."

"Okay." I replied because I knew not to go against his authority.

. . .

MY EYES FELL onto the towels that laid on the bed and I knew they were for me. I picked up the items and headed towards the bathroom. Before I made it inside, Lenox called out to me. "Make sure you wash that thang good because it's time I taste it. You're eighteen now Pure." he spoke with so much lust in his eyes. My insides began to instantly quiver because I never thought this day would come. I always thought that Lenox just wasn't into me, and I was fine with that. However, all this time he was waiting for me to turn eighteen. *Ain't this about a bitch,* I thought as my legs trembled. I don't know about these other bitches but Lenox wasn't attractive to me. Don't get me wrong, he was in his mid-forties and handsome but he had this creep demeanor about him. So trust me, when he didn't bother to sleep with me, I was happy. I guess that's what I get for being so naive. *Sigh.*

2

Mic Check 2

YUNG BABY

"Baby! Baby! Baby! Baby!
      Baby! Baby! Baby! Baby!"

HEARING the crowd scream my name made a nigga feel good. I was backstage with my mic in my hand bouncing around to amp myself up. I patiently waited for the beat to drop and my DJ shouted over the mic "WELCOME HOME YUNG BABYYYY!" the crowd began to scream; it was now time. I ran from backstage to the front of the stage and the electrified yells made my adrenaline pump more.

"Who the fuck missed me?!" I shouted into the mic. Again the crowd went lit.

"Nah, nah, nah, y'all ain't loud enough. I said who the fuck miss the Baby?!"

After receiving the response I was looking for, right on cue, my beat dropped.

"Middle fingers in the air!......FUCK 12! FUCK 12! FUCK, FUCK, FUCK 12 !"

. . .

I BEGAN SPITING the lyrics to my song titled *Fuck 12*. I had recorded the track right before I got locked up so it was perfect timing with my release. My crowd was so turnt I don't know if they were feeling my shit or if they were happy to see me. I had been gone 2 long years, and I was back to regain my crown in the industry. I had a solid ass team who was now on stage with me, and while I was locked up, we signed a female artist by the name of Olivia Luv. Not that the industry wasn't ours already, but it was time we came with some new shit and take over like Young Money. I had some dope ass features and speaking of one she was coming out now.

THE BEAT SWITCHED and an artist by the name of *Barbie Amor* ran to the stage. Barbie was my boy's Dinero's artist so me and her met on several occasions. She was mad cool and ah nigga ain't gone lie, if I didn't know Dinero was hitting that, I would try my hand. Her ass was a big ass flirt, but she wasn't fucking with me.

I WATCHED Barbie as she went in on the lyrics to her song titled Milk Mike https://youtu.be/c0l754Go0ug and I could tell this was one of her favorite songs because she fell into a zone rapping. I ran over to her side, stood by her and helped her sing the ad-libs.

MILK MIKE, Milk Mike, I'm in love with him,
    I hold his strap for him in case a nigga trip on him.
    Milk Mike, Milk Mike, he make that dick squirt,

He a beast in the streets and under the skirt.

AFTER THIS TRACK, we dropped our song we had together and the crowd really went crazy. It was another lovey dovey ass song for the ladies and by their reaction they were feeling it. This would be our last song because I still had a couple tracks with Million, one of my other artists who was more like my brudda. Mill did most of the recording and engineering. He also handled all the paperwork and important shit with BBE.

RIGHT NOW I FELT GOOD. I felt like the man. I couldn't wait for this moment, and I was happy as fuck because I was getting the exact reaction I needed. *The world is mine.* I bowed my head as Mill ran out onto the stage. This was only the beginning and I didn't plan on stopping any time soon.

$$$

"DADDYYYY!" Emani screamed and ran towards me full speed. Although I had spent this morning with her she was still excited to see me.

"What's up ma, why you still up?"

"I was watching you on TV with mommy." she replied with a giggle.

"You liked daddy performance?" I asked walking her back to her room. I bypassed Tristian who was sitting on the sofa with her head buried into her phone. She was still mad that a nigga came home and didn't fuck her, but I told her ditsy ass I wasn't fucking her. Keep it real, I ain't had no pussy yet because I slept with my daughter then left straight for the show.

"You and Barbie sure look mighty cozy on stage." Tris appeared in the doorway.

"Man that's my nigga Dinero girl. I don't even get down like that baby girl. But since you tryna be funny, I wish Barbie fine ass would let a nigga wife her." she smacked her lips and stormed out of the room.

"Mommy mad." Mani giggled making me laugh.

"Yeah baby, she be trippin." I laughed along with her and kissed her on the forehead. "It's time for bed baby girl."

"Where you going?"

"I'm going home. But I'll be back later."

"Okay. I'mma stay up and wait for you."

"No Mani, it's late and you gotta go to bed."

"But I always stay up late. Mommy and Olivia lets me stay up."

Olivia? I thought to myself. To my knowledge, Tris couldn't stand Liv but shit I guess while I was gone they got cool.

"I'll wake you up in the morning."

"You not going back to jail right daddy?" My daughter pulled my attention back to her. I shook my head because this was the shit her mother had fed her. When I left, Mani was only three and had just learned to talk. Now her ass was talking up a storm. Each time I talked to her on the phone, or she would visit me, we told her I was in the army.

"No baby. Daddy not ever leaving you again okay."

"Okay. I love you." she ran over to her bed and climbed underneath her Dora bed set. Just that fast she tuned me out because she grabbed her remote to finish watching a recording of Dora. It was crazy how she was still obsessed with Dora after all these years but it was cool cause Mani swore she knew Spanish.

"Good night. I love you too." I told her but she ignored me. I headed out the door and went to holla at Tris.

"Tris y'all good, y'all need anything?"

"No we're okay. I still got some money from the account you set up."

"Aight." I nodded. And this was a reason I respected my baby moms. She wasn't like these sack chasing hoes out here and that's the one thing I hated, a scheming ass hoe.

"Can I get some dick?" she looked up with a smirk. Before I could reply, she hit me with "It's been 2 years Baby." when I looked at her she dropped her head.

"So you mean to tell me you ain't fuck nobody since a nigga been gone?"

"Just fuck me and see." she said and no lie, a nigga dick got brick hard. I looked at her one last time and slightly shook my head.

"Come on man." I told her and bust a U to head into her bedroom. Before I walked out, I could see the smile that crept up on her face. I hope she didn't make this shit no habit because a nigga wasn't rocking with her like that.

$$$

AFTER FUCKING the life back into Tris, I felt rejuvenated so I left to head to the studio. Just that fast she begin to act clingy asking was I coming back. Because of all the time I spent away from my daughter, I agreed to come back and spend the day with them tomorrow. There was work that needed to be done, so I knew this was gonna be a long ass night.

WHEN I WALKED into the studio, I was met with a cloud of smoke. The air was filled with weed smoke and Black and Mild. The Black and Mild smoke came from Bang because that nigga couldn't live without blacks. There were a few chicks inside but being the cocky nigga I was I didn't bother to acknowledge them. I headed over to greet Olivia, and we began chopping it up.

"I'm so happy you back." Olivia smiled making me smile along with her.

"Me too. Shit gotta get done round here."

"Million been holding it down but ain't nothing like having the boss around." she batted her eyelashes. Olivia was head over heels in love with a nigga. When she first became part of the team I was locked up, but she made it her business to always visit me. Olivia was pretty as fuck but I wasn't into mixing business with pleasure. I knew how that shit went. I give her this dope dick and she starts tripping. Right now a nigga was just getting back on a grind, so I wasn't looking for love. I was single and the closest thing to a bitch I had was my baby mama. However, I wasn't fucking with her like that either.

"WE GOT CRAZY GIRLZ THIS WEEKEND." Million walked over to us and handed me a flyer.

"Shit, you know I'm with it." I dropped the flyer onto the table and focused in on him. "What's been shaking bro?"

"Tryna keep shit going while you were locked up. I got

20

some dope ass shit lined up too. Got an interview with Power in 2 weeks and the BET awards next month. We gone rip BET Experience first then we go up for an award."

"You just so certain we gone win. Nigga we going up against Cardi for best collaboration."

"What that mean? Nigga, don't doubt yo'self; the world loves you." he wasn't lying. I had the fans on my side because I genuinely indulged with them. I was this same way before I left, and I was gone do the same now that I was back.

"Liv, you up." Bang said stepping from inside the booth. He walked up on me and we pounded fist.

Bang was another one of my artists but another brother. He really wasn't heavy into rapping like me because he was more of a guard. I say that because no matter where we went he kept his strap and watched the crowd better than the hired security. Bang was the hot headed nigga on the label while Million was the more level-headed one. Which is why I left Mill to run my shit while I was gone. For the rest of the night, I chopped it up with my team, and we continued to discuss our next show. We were gonna rock *Crazy Girlz* strip club so this was gonna be a little fun. The strip club shows were always my most laid back and right about now, I needed to see some thick bitches clapping asses.

3

Mic Check 3

BLAKE 'PURE SEDUCTION' BAILEE

"Why you looking like that Blake?"

"Just nervous that's all."

"Well bitch you better snap out of it because it's some money in the building. Baby fine ass here with his crew. They go on at 1, and after, they gonna head up to the VIP. Bitch you better get it together." Cori looked up from lacing her shoe to give me that same look she had been giving me for the last three days.

It was my third day, and I was a wreck. I was still a bit nervous because I didn't think I danced as good. I mean, I knew how to dance but I didn't know how to work the pole like most girls. Now don't get it twisted, Cori had showed me a cool little move to do that didn't require the pole. But I still wanted to climb that bitch to the roof because that's when the money showers came.

Since the first day I started, which was 4 days ago, Cori had been the only one to really make me feel at home. It's like everywhere I went bitches threw shade and the shit was starting to get on my last nerve. I was a real laid back but cool chick. Just like back at home I was there to get my money. I didn't have beef with nobody. I really didn't play too much into people and what they had going on because I had to figure out my own damn life. This wasn't the life for me and it hadn't been since I got sold. However, I didn't have a plan nor a damn ID because I was still a minor before I went to jail.

Sitting in that cell gave me enough time to think about my life and working for Lenox wasn't it. I had to figure out a way to escape without the nigga trying to kill me. Them other chicks in the house loved that shit. They didn't have no hope, no education, and they were comfortable being owned. Being with Lenox, he owned every part of you. He told us when to eat, how to dress and would mentally abuse us like he was on some R Kelly shit.

"You up ma!" Cori said snapping me from my thoughts. I looked at her then back to the ground. I finished tying up my thigh high boots and stood to my feet.

"You a bad muthafucka Blake. Stop pouting and shit like a little ass girl and go own that fucking stage. These bitches ain't got shit on you in here. So what you can't work the pole, you sexy as fuck and that's all that matters." I turned to look from Cori and let out a soft sigh. She walked out the room to take the stage because she was gonna collect my money for me.

LOOKING over my outfit I had to admit I was looking cute. I was wearing a white once piece that only covered my nipples and the bottoms was made into boy shorts. I had on my thigh high boots to match and my makeup was natural with a gold smoky eye to match. Courtney had done my hair in a bunch of flowy curls. I applied another coat of lip gloss on my lips and right then the DJ called out to me.

Tonight the club was packed because Yung Baby was performing. Although I wasn't moved like the other girls I had to look my best. Yung Baby was a hot artist that had a serious buzz. He was the shit before he went to jail but since he'd been back it seems like that's all everyone talked about. Even the girls back at home listened to his music and always talked about how fine he was. This was gonna be my first time seeing him in person, and that's if I get the chance. These bitches were swarming the floor so it was a possibility I may not see him.

"Bringing to the stage, this has become one of my favorites. Fellas, get yo dollars out and make some noise for Pure Seductionnnn!"

HONESTLY, I'm tryna stay focused
  You must think I've got to be joking when I say
  I don't think I can wait
  I just need it now
  Better swing my way

I STEPPED out onto the stage with my most seductive stroll. Summer Walker *Girls Need Love* played from the speakers and it was something about this song that put me in a zone. I began doing a sexy dance before walking over to the edge of the stage. As I went down slowly into the splits I could feel the entire club's eyes on me. I closed my eyes for a split-second and pretended I was the only one in the room. When the men began screaming, it brought me from my trance. Already it had begun to rain on me and when I noticed the nigga in the front who was throwing the money I walked over to him. He looked like a dope boy with all the gold he wore. His diamonds lit up the room along with his watch.

I looked at him and began fucking him with my eyes. I had him right where I wanted him because he didn't take his eyes off of me as he continued to throw his money. I don't know why, but I could feel eyes on me. I looked up towards the VIP balcony and I locked eyes with Yung Baby. His hands rested on the banister and his eyes were trained on me. His fitted hat sat at the top of his head and just like the guy in front of me, he was iced the fuck out.

I quickly broke eye contact by laying back. I lifted my legs into the air and made my heels clap along with my ass. I did this for a few moments then turned over doggy style. I used this as my chance to slide out of my outfit. Now fully naked, I slithered my way towards the pole and this was my chance to own the room. I reached my hand out for the pole and, when I knew I was in position, 1, 2, 3...I flipped myself over so my ass could touch the cold steel. I was slightly in a handstand. I spread my legs and suddenly the crowd erupted and money began to fly through the air. *Gottem*, I thought glad that I had succeeded. This move was hard, so I always said a quick prayer before doing it.

Standing to my feet, I didn't bother looking into the crowd. I walked off-stage trying to catch my breath and headed for the dressing room. When I walked in, I walked over to Cinnamon and grabbed her bottle of Hennessy. I was in major need of a drink, so I took a huge gulp.

"You did good baby." Cin patted my ass and smiled.

"Thank you. It's crazy you and Cori say that because I always doubt myself."

"Well stop bitch. You good as fuck." she said making me feel better.

Knowing someone was walking in, Cin and I looked up. It

was Champagne ol hating ass. She looked at me then to Cin and rolled her eyes. It was crazy because me and the bitch lived together but acted like total strangers at work. Not that we got along at home but you would think it would be us against all these other hating ass bitches. Nah, the same way she did me at home she did me at work. However, each time, I brushed her ass off. I knew sooner or later me and Champagne was gonna rumble, and I was ready. I was growing tired of this bitch.

"SEDUCTION! YOU WANTED IN THE VIP." One of the bottle girls walked in and said.

"The VIP?"

"Bihhhh, Baby want you, so you betta go wash up and get that money. You lucky." Cin said just as Cori walked in and handed me my bag of money.

"Thanks babe." I told her and began stuffing the money into my backpack. The entire bag was full so tonight I had racked up. I knew Lenox would be happy and at the end of the day this was all that mattered.

"Girl, he wants you so what you gone do?" The bottle girl asked and I could hear Champagne smack her lips.

"Fuck you smacking your lips for. Yo ass always hating." Cin shot at Champagne.

"Don't hate because my bitch bomb" Cori had to add her two cents.

"Ain't nobody worried about this hoe." Champagne shot with sarcasm in that *hoe*. Nobody knew my background so that bitch was trying to be funny. Cin and Cori were cool as fuck but that wasn't a part of my life I was proud of.

"I'm cool." I replied to the bottle girl shocking the entire room.

"Bitch is you crazy?" Cori shot with her face frowned.

26

"I'm just not pressed for him. You go."

"He didn't ask for me. Trust me, if he did I'd be up there."

"Well I'm cool." I headed to the back to go shower and change. I was still gonna head out to get some lap dances but I refused to go to that damn VIP. Like I said, I wasn't pressed about the nigga and his crew. People confused my hoeing for sack chasing and sack chasing wasn't in me. Period.

4

Mic Check 4

YUNG BABY

As we made our way out the VIP towards the stage I passed by ol girl who had just got off the stage. She was giving some old nigga a lap dance and when she saw me, she quickly dropped her head. I continued for the stage and grabbed the mic from the DJ. I began talking into the mic to hype the crowd and with my presence alone I did just that. Mill was holding the bread, so he could make it rain on em and like always Bang was on his P's. I did a few songs and held the crowd down. By the time we were on our last song Liv emerged from the back and the beat dropped to *Pull Up On Me*. Liv began singing the hook as I bopped my head in tune with the track.

PULL UP in my VIP and let me see sum'n,
If you ain't fucking me with then let me know sum'n.
I been feeling you so let me sum'n,
Tonight it's me and you so we gone fuck sum'n

. . .

I BEGAN to spit my verse and I made sure to look over at shorty who was now standing up watching the stage. I don't know why, but baby stole the show tonight just like she was stealing my attention. Not only was her performance dope, but she was bad as fuck. She wasn't the typical bad; she had more of a young and sexy sex appeal to her. She looked innocent as fuck and I don't know why, but this didn't seem like the place for her. It's like her eyes held some type of repentant and I definitely wanted to fuck.

When Mill walked up on me and wrapped his arm around my neck, he stole my attention from ol girl. I was on my last verse but a nigga mind wasn't even here. Once we were done, we headed back towards the VIP. I scanned the room for ol girl and when I found her she was talking to some other chick by the bar. I walked over to her, and I could see her body tense up.

"WHAT HAPPENED TO YOU SHORTY? Didn't they tell you I asked for you up top. Why you ain't pull up on me?"

"Umm, I, Uhhh. I'm just not interested." she replied taken me aback. Before I could say another word to her, another dancer stepped up and got all in a nigga face. This was the same bitch that had been on me all night.

"You must be ready to suck some dick?" I asked, making sure ol girl heard me. When I turned around, I knew she heard me because her facial expression went from tense to irate. Just seeing her like this, made me grab the other chick's hand and take her upstairs. I wasn't into begging no bitch and especially not a stripper.

$$$

"MAN JUST WATCH OUT." I shoved ol girl from off of me because the bitch couldn't even get my dick hard. She had been sucking my dick for nearly thirty minutes and my shit was still soft as doctor cotton.

"It ain't my fault you on drugs."

"Bitch, ion't do drugs. Get yo silly ass out of here hoe." I shoved that bitch so hard she went stumbling back. She was lucky I didn't knock her ass down the stairs.

The only reason I didn't was because I didn't want to get hit with a lawsuit. Tired of the club scene, I motioned for my niggas so we can roll. As we crossed the threshold of the club, me and baby girl locked eyes for a third time tonight. Because of how she did a nigga I frowned and turned my head on some *fuck you* shit. We headed out the club and a nigga ain't look back. However, for some reason, she was on my mind heavy.

Lil mama was sexy as fuck. She had a soft brown complexion with the perfect nose. Her eyes were innocent and that's what stood out the most. Her hair was in curls and even if it wasn't hers the shit looked good. She was about 5'5 in height, with a slim thick body frame. Although she had ass, she still had a small frame that was perfect.

Being in this industry, all types of bitches came my way. I'm talking from exotic to urban. Baby girl wasn't all exotic looking like Tris, but to me she was perfect as a mutha-fucka. Just because of how she played me, I was gone make her suck my dick and shove her ass out my way like the last stripper hoe. Like I said, I didn't chase bitches. Shit, I didn't have to. I was that nigga in my city and every bitch wanted me.

. . .

"AYE NIGGA, you still mad bout that bitch?" Bang asked sensing my mood change.

"Hell yeah, that bitch couldn't suck dick for shit. A nigga fresh out and wanted some fire ass head." he burst out laughing making me laugh along with him. I was serious shit. I hadn't got no head yet and pussy wasn't good enough.

"That little bitch *Seduction* was bad." Bang looked into the air like he was fantasizing about her. *Seduction,* I laughed to myself because this nigga remembered her name. I knew he was on her because he went and tipped her a good ten gees. He didn't tip not one bitch but her. I can't front, if I wanted to, her set was dope. Especially when she did that handstand with the splits.

"I can't wait to fuck."

"Nigga you ain't fucking."

"Why not?"

"Because I'm fucking first." we both fell out laughing. When he looked in another direction I assumed she had stepped out the club.

"We gon see about that." Bang walked away from me and headed over to ol girl. Right then, another stripper walked up on me and I instantly took in her appearance. She was another one that was bad as fuck. Now this one was exotic as fuck and I had noticed her talking to ol girl that was playing with a nigga.

"You like my friend huh?" she asked smiling. A part of me wanted to curse her ass out but for some reason she seemed cool.

"Nah, she a kid. And I could tell because she playing with a nigga." I looked over to ol girl, and she was talking to Bang. The way she was giggling had me feeling kinda unsettled.

"She's really cool. And yes, she's young; that's my baby.

But real shit, she not like these other hoes. She does this to pay bills and not sack chase."

"That's what's up." I smiled and for some reason I got the same impression. "What's her name? And don't give me that stripper shit."

"Blake." she began giggling making me laugh with her.

"Blake. I like that." I rubbed my chin and again I turned to look at her. "And what's your name?"

"I'm Cori." she extended her hand to me.

"Nice to meet you Cori. You cool as fuck."

"Just a real chick." she nodded her head and looked over in Blake's direction. "Well I gotta roll. Come back and see us." she said and winked.

"Fasho ma." I smiled and headed for the bus. Because we were doing a local tour, we drove the bus to all our events. I actually liked it better because I was able to chill, watch TV and pop bottles.

WALKING to the back of the bus, just as I figured, Tay, one of my crew members had some bitches already on the bus. Not wanting to be bothered, I turned back around and headed back to the front. I slid into my seat and pulled out my phone to busy myself. I don't know why, but I had to get another glimpse at Blake who was still talking to Bang. Although they were indulged in a conversation her eyes were trained on the bus. She couldn't see inside because of our tint, but she watched the bus hard. I laid my head back and began fucking around on social media. Shortly after, Bang walked onto the bus and when the driver closed the doors I knew he was the last nigga we waited for.

"She ain't fucking with me." he looked over at me with a stupid ass grin.

"Duh nigga. She ain't fucking with me, so I know she

ain't fucking with yo fat ass." we both laughed. I always cracked on Bang because he was a big nigga. Don't get me wrong; he wasn't all sloppy and shit. He just had a big ass baller belly that went with his stature. Bang was a fly nigga. All the niggas on my label and in my crew was fly. Bang pulled bitches left and right. But like I said, if she wasn't fucking with me, she damn sure wasn't giving that nigga no play.

"Ion't give a fuck, I got her fine ass homegirl number. Cori. With her thick ass." again we both laughed because this nigga was crazy. Cori was fine as fuck though. We began shooting our shit as we made our way to the studio. Tomorrow we had a day time party at The Rooftop on Wilshire Blvd. The event was at 3:00PM, so I was gonna make sure I got some rest. Once we got to the studio, I was gonna head home to my crib out in Hollywood Hills. Sometimes I hated going to that crib because the shit was lonely as fuck.

I had 6 bedrooms and didn't have much company. Well, other than Bang. That nigga always stayed at my crib because he too was a lonely muthafucka. And this is why I always stayed at Tris house because over there I had a family. However, I haven't been to my crib since I been home so tonight I was taking my ass home.

5

Mic Check 5

BLAKE 'PURE SEDUCTION' BAILEE

On the drive home, I played around on my phone to kill time. My Uber driver was quiet as hell which was odd because every driver I had was always talkative. When we pulled up, I noticed Champagne's car out front which told me she had beat me home. Normally she went on dates after the club and because she was here already I frowned. Bitch didn't even bother giving me a ride home. I couldn't wait until I got my own car. Lenox had promised the minute I was released and turned 18 he was gonna get me a car but I needed to get my license.

THANKING MY DRIVER, I quickly jumped out of the car and made my way to the door. I had already text Lenox to tell him have the door unlocked so I was able to head right in. Locking the door behind me, the house was pitch black so I walked in careful not to bump into the glass table. As I was heading for my room.

Pap!

I flew into the hallway wall and grabbed my stinging face.

"Bitch, have you lost your fucking mind!"

Bop!

Lenox's voice roared as he punched me in the face and this time I hit the ground. He walked up on me and stood over my body and began punching me repeatedly. I balled up in a fetal position, so he wouldn't connect with my face. Tears began to pour from my eyes because every jab hurt. Not only that, but I didn't know what I had done so bad to deserve this abuse.

"Get yo funky ass up and go take a shower. We ain't done with this!" he shouted, but I was too scared to move. "Get the fuck up!" I jumped to my feet and stormed into my room. I was still crying so hard I could barely pull out my clothing to shower in.

WHEN I WALKED into the restroom, the first thing I did was look at my face in the mirror. I had a gash under my chin and my eye was swollen. Just seeing my eye made me cry harder. I began to have flashbacks of when my mother used to whoop my ass. See, my mother was smart. Because I had to go to school, she made sure to beat me in places that would be hidden under my clothes. Never in my life had I had a black eye or any abuse to my face. Regardless, I was having the same heart wrenching pain I had when I lived with her. Lenox had never put his hands on me but since I had finally slept with him I guess things had changed.

The day I was released from jail, is the day Lenox aggressively abused my body. Not only did he fuck me in every hole, he made me suck his dick until he nutted down my throat. Since that day, sex with Lenox had become a regular. I used to think I was the special one, but that shit had gone out the window. I was now just like all the other girls in the home. I was Lenox's sex slave, prostitute and now his punching bag.

I stepped into the shower and let the water run over my abused body. When it came time to soap up, I flinched with every rub because my body was sore as hell. Once I was done, I staggered into my bedroom. I didn't even have the strength to dress. Instead, I climbed under my cover and cried myself to sleep. I was so heartbroken at this very moment and, for the first time, I regretted leaving my mother's home. I mean it's not like I had a choice. I could have run away but where the hell would I have gone?

$$\$\$\$$$

THE NEXT MORNING, I tried to open my eyes but my left eye was closed completely. My body was so sore I could barely move. The sound of pounding on my door, is what woke me up, but I was too embarrassed to face whoever it was. Scared that it was Lenox, I shot up and unlocked it.

"What the fuck happen to your face?" Courtney frowned with concern. When she reached for my eye I flinched from the pain. "Lenox did this huh?" she asked and I shook my head yes. She began shaking her head as she told me to come eat breakfast. I walked over to my bed and slid into something quickly because Lenox hated when we were late for breakfast.

BY THE TIME I walked in, all the ladies were seated

around the table. The first person I locked eyes with was Champagne and the bitch had a sly smirk on her face. I looked over at Courtney and her arms were crossed over the other as she stared at me with murder in her eyes. When Lenox walked in, he took his normal seat at the head of the table and all hell broke loose.

"Look at her muthafucking face!" Courtney shouted in Lenox direction. He looked over at her as if she had lost her everlasting mind. "You should be ashamed of your fucking self Lenox. It's bad enough you got her selling pussy for you but she is a fucking baby!" the room was silent as everyone looked on nervously. Lenox stood to his feet and walked over to where Courtney sat.

Wham!

He backhanded her so hard she fell out the chair and grabbed her face. Tears began to pour from my eyes because I wanted to help her so bad but I couldn't. Still holding her face she lifted up to take her seat. Court was better than me because she took that hit like a gee.

"SINCE YOU WANNA TAKE up for this hoe bitch you better walk in here with 10 gees tonight. This bitch had a chance to go up in VIP with Yung Baby, and she declined. Do you know how much money this bitch turned down?" he shot me a look of disgust. I couldn't help but look at Champagne and just like I figured the bitch had a smirk on her face. I knew it was her that told on me because we were the only two working the club. I swear I couldn't wait to that day came when I beat her ass.

"Now if any one of you bitches feel like y'all too good and y'all pass up this kind of money, then you're gonna be looking like this hoe right here. I spend too much damn money feeding, clothing and keeping a roof over y'all head to pass up any type of money."

EVERYONE REMAINED quiet and listened to Lenox go on and on. I had fallen into a complete zone so everything he said was a blur. My mind drifted off to last night and this was the only thing I had to make me smile inside. The way Yung Baby approached me had me slightly smitten. I knew I probably blew my chance but just knowing he chose me over every girl in the room made me feel superior.

Yung baby was not only handsome, he also possessed a swagger out of this world. He stood about 6 feet, with the sexiest chocolate skin. He wore his hair low with waves and connecting sideburns. Although he had a baby face, with a dimple, everything about him screamed grown ass man. The way he walked through the crowd he demanded everyone's attention. He was also a very talented rapper, and he made music for the ladies. The song he had done last night called *Pull Up On Me* was so dope. It was some-thing about the way he looked at me while rapping that had me stuck in a trance.

"Pure, when you done go to the room." Lenox said bringing me from my thoughts.

"Okay." I replied and dropped my head back down to my plate. I began picking at my food as I searched my mind for my last thoughts of Yung Baby. I was tryna do everything to take my mind off this table and especially Lenox.

6

Mic Check 6

YUNG BABY

3 weeks later...

"A, HIT CORI FOR ME."

"For what nigga so you can ask about Blake ass?"

"Man mind yo business." I laughed and watched as Bang pulled out his phone and dialed Cori's number. When she answered he passed me the phone.

"Cori what's the deal ma?"

"Hey bro?" she sounded excited to hear from me. Over the last few weeks Bang and Cori were kicking it tough. She had come to the studio a couple times and each time she would always walk in with food. Cori was growing on me each day and I swear she was becoming like a sister to the label. Not only her being cool, her ass was a fucking gangsta. She kept a pistol and had a mouth on her.

"What's up with my baby girl?"

"I don't know. I texted her a few times, and she hasn't hit back. She hasn't even been to the club."

"Damn I wonder what's up with her?"

"Your guess is as good as mine. If I knew where she stayed I'd swing by for you but I don't know shit. She kinda private."

"Yeah I understand. Well if her ass come through hit me but don't tell her."

"Man give my shit ol sprung ass nigga. Blake don't want yo uglass." Bang said punching my shoulder.

"Fuck you hoe." I passed him the phone before he had a fit.

"What's up baby." he tried to whisper into the phone. He stood up from his seat and walked away so his ass could simp.

"Talking bout I'm sprung." I shook my head laughing. This nigga was open for Cori so he couldn't talk.

"MILL WHAT'S UP? A nigga hungry as fuck." I told Mill as he walked from inside the booth. He was laying a track to his *Legacy* album. Nigga had been in here working for 2 days without even washing his ass. I couldn't say I blamed him because we were Trap Rappers. We bled the studio like a trap house.

"Hell yeah I ain't ate since yesterday."

"Aight. Take a break my nigga. Let's head out to *Hot & Juicy*." I grabbed my bag.

"Aye lover boy, let's roll!" Mill called out to Bang who was in the corner on some real Romeo shit. Tay, who did a lot of engineer work, heard Mill and flew his ass out the room along with Hunchie one of our other niggas.

"Damn, niggas is starving." I laughed at how everybody nearly killed themselves tryna get out of the room.

WE ALL MADE our way for the Bus and waited on our

driver to come down. The driver, Craig, lived upstairs from the studio. The whole unit was mines, so I stationed him upstairs. When I first met Craig he was actually homeless. He was Tris cousin on her pops side and the only family she had out here in Cali. When I asked the nigga what could he do, he mentioned drive trucks so that told me he had a class A license. I bought the bus, made him our driver and gave the nigga somewhere to lay his head. I fucked with Craig heavy because he was about his coins. No matter what time of the day, that nigga would reply to his text and come right down to handle his business.

WHEN WE PULLED up to the restaurant, Tay headed inside to let them know we were here. Per usual they were gonna sit us outside on the deck so we wouldn't be bothered with fans while we ate. About 15 minutes later, Tay came back and motioned for us to head inside. We bypassed all the people who watched us in awe and made our way outdoors. I tried to move fast so no one would notice me. When it came to my food, I liked to eat in peace. Especially my seafood. I wanted to crack crab in peace. I loved the fuck out of seafood, and I was my mother's child fasho. This was her favorite spot. Anytime I got the chance I picked her up for lunch and brought her here. Even if I was too busy to bring her, I would send someone to get it and drop it off to her. And each time she would call me all excited.

Speaking of moms, I needed to swing by and give her the bread for our up and coming family reunion. Because we had a big ass family our shit would always go up. I was an only child but my grandma had 12 kids. Out of those 12 each of them had four to six kids except my moms. Me and mom dukes were hella close but because she worked so much her ass was always busy. It was pretty much just the two of us since most of my family was back in Atlanta.

Atlanta is where my grandma moved to a couple years ago. She moved away to be with her new husband who worked out there. Everyone else in the family was pretty much spread out all over the globe. Me and moms were the only two here in our hometown other than my cousin Brianna. Therefore, I copped my mom a couple businesses and her ass insisted on working. She opened three Gyms, a Spa and her favorite was a Boutique that sells exclusive handmade clothing. Most of the time she would sew the shit up herself. It was crazy because when I first got my deal I asked her what she wanted. I thought she would say a house or car, but instead she said a sewing machine. Imagine my surprise when she told me it cost 40 bands. I didn't trip though because I had received a million dollar sign-on bonus.

"AIN'T that the stripper chick that shot you down?" Mill said pointing over to the corner. When I looked in the direction he pointed, my eyes fell onto Blake little ass. I guess she felt us watching her because she finally looked over and locked eyes with me. I looked her up and down and the dress she wore was inappropriate for my liking. She had on a short ass black dress like she was walking around the club. The dress was so short her cheeks were nearly hanging off the seat. She quickly dropped her head because my face frowned up. I looked over at her date and the nigga looked old enough to be her pops. He wore a cheap ass suit and it was evident he was some cornball ass old nigga.

"Yeah, that's his wifey." Bang laughed. I really wasn't in the joking mood right now so I picked up my menu and began browsing like I didn't already know what I wanted. Shortly after, Blake and her granddaddy got up to leave and Bang stupid ass just had to say some shit.

"Blake, bring yo fine ass here girl." she looked over and I could tell she was embarrassed. She walked over to us, but she made sure to walk around the other way so she wouldn't be behind me. "Why yo ass ain't been to work? We coming up there this weekend girl."

"Okay." she giggled and walked off. I didn't bother to look up. Instead I focused on the menu like she didn't exist. Seeing her with that old nigga, I began to wonder if he was one of her tricks from the club or was she on some escorting shit. Most of the strippers I knew indulged in that shit and if that was the case I really didn't want her ass now. Stripping was one thing but selling yo self was prostitution. Damn, I really was checking for little baby so a part of me prayed he was her pops or something.

"What's up y'all?" I looked up and Olivia was taking a seat.

"Sup Liv." everyone greeted her but me. I didn't mean to be rude but I had shit on my mind.

"What's up Baby?" she shot sarcastically in my direction.

"Sup ma?"

"Why you looking like that? What's wrong with you?"

"He just caught his little stripper bitch cheating on him." Bang laughed like shit was funny.

"That ain't my bitch nigga. She fa everybody." I shot at him and directed my attention elsewhere.

"I knew she looked familiar." Liv said, so I assumed she saw her walking out.

"I don't know why you fronting nigga. You like little mama so you need to get her." Mill said adding his two cents. I wished these niggas would just shut the fuck up.

When I looked up in his direction, I caught a mug from Liv like she was a bit jealous. And this is exactly why I wouldn't fuck her. She always hated on bitches that I brought around and I hadn't even gave her the impression I wanted her. Before I could check Mill ass, the waitress walked over and began taking our order.

"I'm ordering first; fuck these niggas." I told her and she cracked a smile. She walked over to me and began taking my order while everyone laughed at my sarcasm.

ME: what's Cori number?

I SHOT Bang a text from across the table. He looked up at me, but he didn't laugh like usual. He sent the number and continued his conversation with the crew.

BANG: (323) 583-1011

ME: aye Sis, I just saw yo girl. What's up with her? She was with some old nigga look like he could be her granddaddy. 💀

CORI: Baby?
  Me: yep
  Cori: 😒 *I finally talked to her today. She said she was coming to work this week.*
  Me: aight good because I'm coming up there. Man I hope she ain't on no hoe shit
  Cori: yo ass is crazy. I'll find out for you.
  Me: good looking 😅

. . .

AFTER I TEXT Cori I sat back and waited on my food. Finally getting over the shit with Blake I joined my crew in a good laugh. We began cracking on Bang since he was the one always cracking jokes. However, the minute our food came the table fell silent and all you could hear was smacking. Every now and then I felt Liv watching me but I ignored her ass. I made a mental note to call Jalani so I could pull up and hit that pussy.

Jalani was just some random chick I fucked with from time to time. She was cute as shit with her head on straight. Jalani didn't care if I came or didn't and that's what I liked. We had an understanding. We fuck and we move on. Just thinking bout that pussy had a nigga dick hard, so I began looking around the table to see how much food these niggas had left. When I noticed everyone was done, I jumped to my feet and rushed out to the bus.

7

Mic Check 7

BLAKE 'PURE SEDUCTION' BAILEE

"Girl, where the hell have you been?" Cori asked the minute I walked into the dressing room.

"I been home. I was sick." I lied. I prayed like hell she wouldn't notice the small gash I still had under my chin. It was still visible but with the help of foundation I was able to cover it. My eye had gone down and my face was back to normal but because my chin was slightly split it took longer to heal.

"Yeah well I almost had to put an APB out on yo ass. You got niggas calling my phone checking for you and shit." she hit me with a smirk.

"WHOOO?" my neck almost popped and a smile crept on my face.

"Baby." again she smirked. I couldn't help but to drop my head but on the inside I was smiling. "Yeah he told me about you on a date with your grandpa." she said and began laughing.

"Oh my goddd. That was not my grandpa." I laughed along with her.

I couldn't front, just knowing he was checking for me made me feel good inside. The night I saw him while on my date, I was embarrassed as hell. And every night since, I thought of that night hoping he didn't know what I really did. The way he looked at me that night, had me confused. Was the nigga mad or checking for me? I was more than sure he was still upset from the night here at the club but just knowing he was checking for me had a bitch feeling good.

"Oh and he's coming tonight." Cori added standing to her feet. The sound of something crashing to the floor made us both turn around. *Damn I didn't know this bitch was here*, I thought looking over at Champagne. I still owed that bitch an ass whooping and because of Lenox she was lucky as fuck. Lenox didn't tolerate fighting each other and that was one of the rules in the house. As much as everyone couldn't stand each other he wanted us to act like one big happy family.

"He really likes you Blake. Just give him a chance." she said pulling my attention from Champagne. "He's a really cool guy." she said as if she had known him her whole life.

"If he comes and want a dance, I'll go up there."

"Mmm, sounds kinda personal to me." Champagne said smacking her lips. Before I could say anything to her, Cori was hot on her shit.

"And you sound like a hating ass bitch to me. I swear I don't like yo ass. Blake ain't gone do shit to you but bitch I'll beat the fuck out yo ass. Keep reaching hoe, keep reaching." Cori sneered then walked out of the dressing room. I shook my head then followed suit before Champagne got a chance to say one word. Once again I wasn't about to entertain this hoe.

. . .

WALKING INTO THE CLUB, I froze in one place. An entourage of niggas was walking through with three huge guards. The first nigga I spotted was the guy that had tipped me last time which was the same one that called out to me at the restaurant. So that told me Baby was amongst the crowd. Scanning the group of niggas, my eyes fell onto him as he swaggered through. His chain swung from side to side and he was looking good.

Close to him was Olivia Luv and I don't know why but the way she looked at me was like she didn't like me. And the only reason she wouldn't like me was more than likely because she was fucking Baby. However, if she was, I couldn't say I didn't blame her. He was very sexy and right now every chick in the room stopped to look in his direction. I quickly turned my head so I wouldn't look thirsty like the rest. I focused in on the stage because the DJ had just announced *Hardcore* which was Cori to the stage.

AS CORI WALKED out to the stage, the club lights went dim and all eyes were on her. The two piece fire red outfit she wore was hella sexy and the girl had moves. Cori was a gorgeous chick and just from her complexion and hair you could tell she was mixed. She had the perfect thick shape with ass out of this world. Not even five minutes into her show, the same guy that had tipped me was now on the stage making it rain on her. The entire dance she stayed in front of him teasing him with her now exposed pussy. When she turned over doggy style she grabbed him from the back and grind her ass on his dick. Something about this dance was hella personal because the fellas couldn't touch us and not to mention, Cori didn't play that shit. Her ass would beat a nigga down for disrespecting her. But nah, this nigga was having his way with her, and she seemed to enjoy it.

AFTER HER SET WAS DONE, I ran to the stage and began scooping her money into the bag. She had already disappeared backstage, so I quickly went to the back to give her money and change my clothes. I was going up next and of course since Baby was here, I was nervous as fuck.

"You did good bitch." I said handing Cori her bag.

"Thank you baby." she smiled.

"Umm, yeah sooo is it something you wanna tell me?" I smirked at her ass just like she always done me.

"Yes, there is." she took a deep breath and looked at me. "Ever since that night, I been kicking it with him. Bang. Well I been kicking it with the whole *Baby Boy Empire*.

"But Bang yo boo?"

"Yes, well no...Man, I don't know. Like, I'm really starting to like him but I don't know." she dropped her head. Yeah, *this shit real,* I thought, because hardcore Cori was being tense.

"Well by the look on his face, he seems really into you. I know it's too soon so don't rush it, but give him a chance hoe." I nudged her arm mimicking the same shit she just told me earlier. A wide smile graced her face then she looked at me.

"I don't love these hoes." again she smirked.

"You get on my damn nerves." I couldn't help but laugh. She often said how she was single and wasn't looking for a nigga because she wanted to get her bread.

However, that was easier said than done. Depending on how *into* her he was, it was only a matter of time before she fell putty in that nigga hands.

"Coming to the stage, fellas get yo dollars out. We have the one, the only, Pure Seductionnnn!" I heard my name being announced. I let out a sigh and headed for the door.

"Good luck." Cori called out to me and I turned around to smile. I continued for the stage and like always, I strutted with all the confidence in the world. No matter how nervous I was, I could vividly hear Cori's voice. "*No matter what, hold yo head up, be confident, and own the fucking room.*"

THE ENTIRE ROOM WENT BLACK, and the single spotlight hit me just as my music dropped.

TWENTY FOUR SECONDS, yeah, you better not stop
You got twenty four seconds, can you beat the shot clock?
What you waitin' on lil' daddy? I ain't got that much time.
You seem anxious, you seem adamant but you ain't press my line

I MOVED around the stage to Ella Mai's *Shot Clock* as I pulled every man in the room eyes on me. I did a sexy little dance then slowly dropped into the splits. I spread my legs wide open as I moved my chest up and down to the beat as if I was performing the song. I began touching myself seductively until the chorus began to play. I then flipped over and went to the pole so I could do my one and only move. The moment I flipped into the handstand, I could feel the money hit my pussy. It's like the men waited for me to do this one move.

I began clapping my ass against the pole then flipped back over into the splits. Suddenly, it's like I could smell his aroma. My heart began to pound as Yung Baby walked over to the stage and began throwing money. With my heart still pounding, I slowly walked over to the side he was on. I began to dance slowly as I looked him in the eyes. This was something we were trained to do, and no matter how many times I did this, right now it was hard. I stepped closer to him so I could lay back and rotate my hips. I had him so gone he leaned into me and whispered in my ear.

"I ain't playing with you tonight Blake. Bring yo ass upstairs and if you don't, I'mma tear this whole club up."

I ACTED unfazed by what he said, so I continued to dance. He threw the last stack at me and his cocky ass walked away. I was glad when the song ended because after that I couldn't even concentrate. I stood up and headed to the back, and just like last time, I needed a damn drink.

WHEN I GOT to the back it was empty. Of course every bitch was out front hoping they got chose by Baby or one of his crew members. I waited for Cori to bring my money then I was gonna head upstairs.

"Let's go hoe." Cori said the minute she walked in.

"Where we going?" I tried to play dumb.

"Girl get dressed and stop playing. Shit I'm just as nervous as you."

"Yeah, yo ass nervous because you like him." I taunted her.

"So why you nervous?" she stopped to look at me and made me burst out laughing. "Exactly, now let's go." she headed to the back so she can take a quick shower.

Following suit, I did the same thing. Baby's words played in my mind and with each thought my heart pounded. I loved the way he took charge. I didn't care about his cockiness. I was still caught up over him choosing little ol me.

8

Mic Check 8

BLAKE 'PURE SEDUCTION' BAILEE

As I headed upstairs to Baby's VIP, Cori hung close to me and we both held a drink. We strutted through the club and all the envy in the room was evident. I guess it spread around the club the last time Baby chose me to come upstairs. Not only that, but that same night he approached me, and then tonight I was the only one he tipped. These bitches were big mad but I didn't pay it any mind. I had a job to do and this shit was only business. I knew it couldn't get too personal because for one, what could a nigga of his status do with me? Two, I was sure he had someone, and three, I had a hidden life behind me. This club shit was just fun and games and a way for me to escape. It was way better than being on the streets and I made pretty great money. Therefore, I was gonna play along. I was more than sure that after tonight I may never even see him again.

WHEN WE MADE IT UPSTAIRS, there were about ten strippers in the VIP and three of them were on Baby. Cori walked over to the girls that were on whose name she said was Bang and said something crazy and it was evident in her body language. Of course, I stayed behind because I wasn't as bold as her and really didn't wanna seem like a hater. Although I was a bit jealous because Caramel started dancing on Baby, and he had a handful of her ass like he enjoyed the view, I played my position. He looked over at me and bit into his bottom lip as she clapped her ass against him. One of his boys grabbed my hand and pulled me over to him. He fell into the sofa, so I began giving him a lap dance trying to take my mind off of what was going on next to me. But it was hard.

Yung Baby's *Clap That Ass* came on, so I began to make my ass clap and his boy started showering me with dollars. When I spent around, Baby's eyes met mine and his face frowned up. This nigga really had his nerves. I spent around so I could avoid his eye connection and continued dancing with his friend.

"You really want me to fuck you up huh ma?" Baby's voice vibrated my neck sending goosebumps down my back.

I slowly turned around and I had to slightly look up to him. *Damn this nigga fine.* I thought as I looked into his deep brown eyes. I don't know what the fuck this nigga was doing to my body, but he had a bitch mesmerized. When he moved, I moved as if he had my body in check. When we got over to the couch, I thought he wanted a lap dance but instead he motioned for me to sit down. *Oh Lord*, I thought because when a nigga asked to sit down it meant they wanted to talk. In this game wasn't no talking or kissing because that shit was too personal. The only man I kissed was Lenox because we all had to kiss him. He said it was a way to connect us together. And under strict orders wasn't no kissing anyone else.

. . .

"WHAT'S a chick like you doing working in a place like this?" Baby asked making me look over to him.

"I don't know. The money I guess." I replied nervously.

"Oh okay." he nodded his head.

"So do you do all the extra shit these other hoes do?"

"Like?"

"Man stop playing with me Blake. You know what the fuck I mean?"

"How do you know my name?" I asked trying hard to change the subject.

"My sis told me." he said and tilted his head to the side.

"Yo sis? Cori?" I asked but I already figured. Especially since she said she had been chilling with them.

"Yeah." he chuckled and his cheek sunk in exposing his dimple. We both got silent for a slight second. "You coming home with me?" he asked catching me off guard. A part of me wanted to scream *hell ye*s but I couldn't. Not only would Lenox kill me if I didn't come home, but I didn't want Baby to look at me like some hoe. Yeah, I know what y'all thinking "bitch you is a hoe" I know, I know, but nah, it's something about him I was intrigued by. And not to mention the question he asked moments ago.

"I don't know Baby. I ummm..."

"You got a nigga? It's cool." he assumed sounding disappointed.

"It's that… it's just...look, I like you. I love the way you keep checking for me so the shit makes you different from the rest of these niggas. With them it's business, but for some reason with you shit seems personal."

"So why you make it seem like it's a bad thing?"

"It is… love don't exist in my world Baby. And yes, I have a husband." I lied because I needed him to leave me alone. This nigga was doing something to me that I

55

couldn't let happen. Without any more words, I stood to my feet. To my surprise, he didn't put up a fight. When I walked over to the banister, I needed to clear my mind but instead, I damn near lost it. I watched as Lenox headed through the crowd as if he was looking for someone. I guess he could feel my eyes watching him because he looked right at me. His face formed into an infuriated frown that instantly made my hands sweat. I was gonna try to hurry down before he came up but when I turned around Baby was standing right in front of me. I looked up into his alluring eyes and I got lost in them forgetting all about Lenox.

"I can have any bitch in this room, but a nigga choose you Blake. I don't know what it is ma, but I gotta have you. You keep running from a nigga but I'mma get you... just wa..." before he could finish, Lenox walked over to us.

"Pure let's go!" I don't know if it was me, but I swear it's like his voice shook the entire second floor. I looked from Baby to Lenox then back to Baby. Everything he had just said still lingered in the air, but Lenox didn't give me a chance to reply.

"Now!" he barked making me look away from Baby. I walked away leaving him standing there but I had to get one last look at him. When I turned around, again our eyes connected but this time, he didn't have those same alluring eyes. They were more like, disappointed and annoyed. However, it wasn't shit I could do. I let out a deep sigh as I followed Lenox down the stairs. Cori had even called my name, but I was too damn scared to turn around. By the time we made it to the door, Champagne was standing there with a smirk and again I knew it was her bitch ass that had to have called him.

$$$

Yung Baby

As me and my crew headed for the exit, Cori was coming out with her bag over her shoulder. I knew what that meant, her ass was rolling out with Bang. When she walked over to me, I knew she was gonna say some shit about Blake but I really didn't even wanna be bothered. I was done chasing shorty. And it was obvious by the look on ol boy face, she really had a nigga. So again, I was gonna let her be.

The moment we stepped out the door, we headed straight for the bus so we could bypass anyone trying to get autographs and shit. Right now a nigga just wanted to get on the bus and prepare for this long ass drive out to Oakland. We had a show at the *Oracle Arena* and it was a huge event. Therefore, I was gonna pass out on the bus until we checked into our rooms. I had been up for two days and a nigga was running off Red Bull and Remy. "Is that Blake?" Cori asked looking across the street in the second lot. I continued to walk until I heard her say "what the fuck." she stopped me in my tracks and made me look across the street. I don't know if I was tripping or not, but it looked like ol boy that came to get Blake out the club had hauled off and slapped the shit out of her. A part of me wanted to keep pushing and mind my business but when I saw that nigga punch her like she was a fucking man, I lost it.

Cori ran full speed towards them, and I was hot on her heels. When I reached them, ol boy had Blake by the neck about to punch her again. When she looked over at me, a nigga heart fell. Her face was bloody and she looked defeated. "This ain't none of y'all business." the nigga said like he was scaring somebody. I whipped my strap out and put it to his head. I knew I couldn't pop the nigga because by now there was a crowd and not only that but the cameras. I swear he better consider today his lucky day.

"Cori take her to the bus."

Cori quickly grabbed Blake then grabbed her purse off the ground. When they walked off I looked back at ol boy.

"Nigga if it wasn't for these cameras, I'd blow yo fucking head off."

"Man this ain't got nothing to do with you. That bitch there belongs to me." he tried to be tough but I could smell the bitch in this nigga.

"Nigga yo bitch just got took." I waited for him to speak but he remained quiet.

"Let's go Baby!" Cori yelled from across the street. When I turned in her direction, Blake had this frantic look on her face. I tucked my strap back into my waistline and focused back on old boy. "It's your lucky fucking day." I seethed then turned to walk away. When I made it across, the girls followed me onto the bus, and we left before the police came.

"Cori we gotta hit Oak in the morn, you rolling?"

"Yeah I got my bag with me." she said pointing to her bag. She was sitting two rows in front of me with Blake and since I sat behind them on the opposite side I could see Blake clearly. She was so in a daze, she looked out the window like a sad puppy. The more I looked at her face, the angrier I became which is why I didn't want to sit by her. I couldn't take seeing her like this. Frustrated, I got up and walked to the back to holla at Million. At times like this, that nigga was the only one I could really holla at. Bang was always on some goofy shit and Tay was just as weird as they come.

"You good my nigga?" Million asked the minute I took a seat.

"Yeah a nigga straight." I said and pulled the blunt from my ear so I could spark it.

"So what you gon do with her?" he asked looking ahead at Blake. Without replying, I took a hard pull from the green and trained my eyes on her. Letting out a sigh, I looked over at Million.

"Real shit Mill, I don't even know."

"You feeling her huh? Be real with me nigga." Instead of replying I nodded my head yes and took the blunt from his hand.

"I don't know what it is about shorty that a nigga digging so hard. I mean she cute as a muthafucka but that ain't just it. It's something bout them eyes. A chick like Blake don't belong in no strip club and by the way ol boy handled her, she don't deserve a nigga like him either."

"You right, just be careful. You don't know her story with that nigga and you got too much to lose bro. Already you done whipped out on the nigga and not to mention it was a crowd of people right there. Lucky we stayed behind so we can make sure muthafuckas wasn't recording."

"Good looking."

"No need, you know I got you. But real shit, see where her head at before you dive in too deep." Mill stood to his feet and headed into the little room we had on the bus that had a bed. I knew he was about to pass out because his eyes were bloodshot red and I could tell he was fighting his sleep. Shit just like me, Mill had been up for days. Bang was the one who slept all the time with his fat ass while Mill and I worked hard. When I looked up front, I saw Cori get up and head over to Bang's seat. I took it upon myself to go check on Blake. She was now wrapped in Bang's blanket, as she still stared out the window.

Sliding into the seat next to her, she turned to look at me. She had a little cut on the side of her eye but nothing too major. It had finally stopped bleeding and I knew it was gonna leave a mark.

"You good ma?" I asked in a low voice.

"Yeah, I'm fine. Thank you again Baby." she looked at me with a pair of glossy eyes.

"I got you. Always." I told her sincerely. "Is that your nigga?" I just had to know. When she nodded her head *yes* I nodded once in agreeance. The nigga looked hella old if you asked me. But I assumed she likes older guys because the guy at the restaurant was old as shit.

"So who the old nigga at the restaurant?" again I just had to know.

"That was… ummm…that was his father." she said referring to her nigga. "So where are we going?" she looked at me and pulled the blanket over her body.

"We heading out to the arena in Oak, so I could do a show. Don't trip, we gone get you some shit from the mall if you don't have shit."

"Okay." she said and looked back out the window. I studied her for a moment trying my best to figure her out. She was kinda standoffish and I didn't know if it was because she didn't know me, or she wasn't interested in me. I mean, she had a nigga like me chasing her ass, and she wasn't fazed. Maybe she was just in love with her nigga. I really don't know what the case was, but after tonight I hoped she wouldn't double back. A nigga that hit a woman was a straight bitch in my eyes. The way he did her and in front of all those people was foul as fuck, so she'd be a fool if she went back.

Finally, getting comfortable, Blake snuggled up underneath me and laid her head on my shoulder. I knew I wouldn't be going to sleep no time soon, so I started going through my many emails. From time to time she would move but each time she went right back to sleep. Once we made it to our destination baby girl and I would for sure have to holla. I wanted to know some things before I just jumped into some shit. The main question I needed answers on was, did her and ol boy stay together and if so where was her family. I mean I know she wouldn't go back to him after this. Well, I hoped she didn't. But these days with women you never knew.

9

Mic Check 9

BLAKE 'PURE SEDUCTION' BAILEE

When I opened my eyes, the sun was peeking through the tints of Baby's bus. I lifted up to stretch and last thing I remembered was Baby sitting next to me. I began looking around and I noticed Cori on one bench and Bang right next to her. I wanted so bad to go find him but I was a bit nervous. Although the sun was peeking through, it was still dark on the bus except for the dim lighting. Building up the courage, I got up and headed towards the back of the bus in hopes I would find him. Everyone was pretty much asleep, so I made sure to tip toe up the aisle as quiet as possible.

When I made it to the back, I noticed a room off to the side. There was a curtain that separated it from the rest of the bus and I knew there was a television back there because of the flicker. Biting into my bottom lip, I pulled back the curtain and Baby was laid back with his feet kicked up on the bed. He tilted his head at me and our eyes met each other. I swear this nigga was so cool.

"Come here lil mama." he said exposing his mouth full of diamonds. I walked in and shut the curtain behind me.

He invited me to lay next to him, and I was happy he did because this bed felt better than that chair. Don't get me wrong, the seats on the bus were comfortable but wasn't nothing like a soft mattress.

"Why you leave me?" I pouted as I snuggled underneath him.

"Man you was knocked out." he chuckled as he ran his fingers through my hair. "This all you?" he asked catching me by surprise. He continued to rub, and I was sure he knew damn well it was because he didn't feel one track.

"Yes." I giggled along because this boy had a sense of humor.

"What you mixed with?"

"My grandmother is full-blown Cherokee Indian."

"And what about yo father side?"

"I don't know my father." I spoke above a whisper. I hated when the subject of a father was ever brought up because I really didn't know the man. My mother was a prostitute and drug addict for as long as I could remember so more than likely my father was one of those tricks she dated.

"Shit I don't either. Fuck both them niggas." he said and I smiled. "So Ms. Blake, Blake... uhhh."

"Bailee." I replied before he called me Johnson or some simple shit.

"Blake Bailee, a nigga like that." he nodded with a slight smile.

"Is Baby your real name?"

"Yep. Baby Taylor."

"Dope name."

"I hated the shit in school. All the girls used to chase me around like *baby, baby*, even the ugly chicks. Shit drove me crazy yo." we both started laughing.

"Well I like it." I smiled and we both got silent. I could

tell something was on his mind, so I waited for him to ask. I became a bit nervous because there is no telling what he had heard.

"So Blake Bailee, what's up ma?"

"Nothing."

"Is that right." he said and like I said I could tell he wanted to ask something. I trained my attention towards the television hoping he would just leave whatever it was alone.

"You live with that nigga?"

"Yes. Why you ask that?"

"Because shit, a nigga just concerned. That's all."

"Thank you." I replied and dropped my head.

When he let out a yawn I knew he was tried. He began fluffing his pillow, so I took it upon myself to snuggle closer to him. He wrapped his arms around me and I couldn't front, the shit felt good. I was looking at the TV, but my mind was in another world. I was really on Yung Baby's tour bus, wrapped in his arms. This was every girl dream and here it was, little ol me, was living it. I didn't know where we would go from here because eventually I would have to go back home. Lenox and the girls were the only family I had. I hadn't talked to my aunt since the day she left me for Texas and I damn sure haven't heard from my mother. Therefore, when he excused me from his presence I wouldn't have a choice but to go back.

$$$

WHEN THE BUS pulled up to the mall, everyone climbed off and headed inside. Like always Yung Baby was in the middle of the pack and to my surprise he had me right by his side. This shit was crazy as fuck. As we headed in so many people were stopping to look at us.

"Aye ma, Gucci cool." he asked as if I was gonna say hell no. I nodded my head yes and he grabbed me around the small of my back. We headed inside Gucci and I kid you not, the nigga bought so much shit. He even went and picked me out a dress.

"You about a size 7?" he asked sizing me up. I blushed because I was exactly a size 7. He giggled slightly and rubbed his chin. "Go try this on." he handed me the dress. Cori was already inside trying on a dress, so I went into the booth next to her and called out to her.

"Here I come." shortly after, she came into my dressing room wearing a cute little dress that showcased all her curves.

"Ooh bitch that's cute." I told her as I slid out my pants. Getting dressed in front of her was normal for us because we were used to the dressing room back at the club. When I was done putting on the dress, I did a little spin in the mirror as Cori admired it.

"Yeah this bomb. I wish I had seen it first." she said checking me out.

"Girl Baby picked it out." I replied and opened the door to see if he approved of how it looked on me. We were going to his show tonight, so I wanted to look my best.

WHEN I STEPPED OUT, he was over to the side talking to two females. His guard and Million stood right by him as he signed I assumed an autograph. I let him handle his business then he looked over at me. He zoomed in on the dress and it's like he fell into a trance. I began fidgeting because I wasn't sure if he liked it or was it too short.

"Yeah that one." his eyes drifted and he smiled. I smiled back at him shyly then walked back into the dressing room. I took the dress off then headed over to him. Just as I made it to him, his phone rang.

"Go find you some heels ma." he told me then answered the call.

"What's up Mani baby?" he said into the phone. I looked over at him and he was smiling wide. A sense of jealousy rushed through my body because all the things he asked me, he failed to mention having a girlfriend. In my feelings, I walked over to the shoes and began searching for a pair to go with my dress.

"Excuse me, can I get this in a size 7."

"Sure, let me check and see if we have your size."

"Thank you." I replied and took a seat. I pretended to be into my phone, so I didn't look out of place just sitting here.

"You find yo shoes?" I heard his voice then felt his presence next to me.

"Yeah." I replied but didn't look over at him. I was still in my feelings.

"What's wrong with you?" he asked sensing the change in my mood.

"Nothing." I shot him a faint smile.

"After this we gon head in Vicky and get you some under clothes. We only out here for two days, so we gone head in Footlocker and you can grab something comfortable for tomorrow."

"Thank you." I looked at him then quickly turned my head.

"Y'all so cute." I looked up to Cori's voice.

"Man don't start yo shit." Baby told her smiling.

"Nah nigga, the way you blew me up over her, I'm starting."

"Oh my god." I blushed and dropped my head.

"Yeah, her ass was dissing a nigga." he looked at me making my heart drop.

"I wasn't dissing you." I blushed again brushing my hair from my face.

"It's smooth, I got you now." he bit his lip and reached over to pinch my cheek.

"Sorry it took so long. Here's your shoe." the lady handed me the heels. Because I didn't need to try them on, I put the one she took out back into the box.

"Let me see them?" Baby asked, so I pulled the shoe from the box.

"Cinderella." he smiled making me and Cori giggle. The shoes did look like something out of the movie. They were plastic with the white tip and white heel. Because they were top of the line, the plastic didn't look cheap. It actually looked like glass.

"Liv at the hotel." Million walked up and said. When Baby respond *okay* he stood to his feet so that was our cue. I handed him the shoes, and he headed for the register.

"I think he really likes you." Cori said smiling.

"I think he really likes his girlfriend." I smirked and headed for the register. Cori was still trying to respond but I didn't want to hear it. She was cool with these niggas, so I knew she would justify for him. Didn't really matter anymore because after this trip I was sure he was kicking me to the curb. Not saying we wouldn't talk anymore, but this nigga had a girl which meant he had another life. And anyway, I was just a prostitute, stripper, hoe, probably in his eyes. Therefore, I wasn't gonna get my feelings wrapped up into him.

10

Mic Check 10

YUNG BABY

"I wanna buy yo love shawty, is you fucking with me?
I gotta bag we could blow so is you fucking with me?"

I HAD the entire stadium on their feet as I performed my song *Buy Your Love*. I chose to do this song because Blake was here tonight and not only that, the ladies loved this shit. Looking out into the crowd it was 75% women in the audience, so I had to please them. I had performed six songs already and this was my last one. It's crazy how there were 19,000 people in this arena but to me it was just me and Blake. From time to time I would look over to the side of the stage just to make sure she was right there. I continued to rock the show and I had the crowd going. By the time I was done with my last song, my adrenaline was pumping because this was another successful night.

WHEN WE RUSHED OFFSTAGE, the crew was still lit. Blake was smiling hard, so I could tell she was impressed. I stopped, so I could sign a few autographs then we headed up the hall for the dressing rooms. When we walked in, we began to take a few pictures, and we were still hyped. Blake took a seat along with Cori and Million had pulled a few other chicks in, who sat on the opposite side. One of the chicks was checking me out so I pulled out my phone and shot Mill a text.

ME: *make sure you get they line*
Mill: *sho*

I SLID my phone back into my pocket and walked over to where Blake and Cori sat. I began chatting with them because I didn't want them to feel left out.

"Y'all ready to roll?"

"Enjoy yo self." Blake said then smirked over to ol girl. She must have peeped us eye fucking each other. *Let me find out she jealous,* I thought looking over to the chick. True she was cute as fuck, but she wasn't fucking with Blake. Shorty was looking like a boss's wife right now and this was a better look than the club. Ignoring Blake, I walked back over to the crew. I told them niggas let's roll because a nigga wanted to finally relax. Not only that, I wanted to chill with Blake in private. I was hoping she let me snatch that dress off her sexy ass but if she didn't I wasn't tripping. I wanted to holla at her to see where her head was at anyway.

A nigga was digging the fuck out of her. Her personality was dope as fuck and the more I was around her I was crushing. Shit was crazy as fuck because ain't no bitch ever had a nigga feeling like this. I felt like a young high school nigga that cracked his first crush. For some reason, I knew

Blake was gone be a handful. Already I almost had to knock a nigga wig back, and real shit, I'll do it all over again.

$$$

WHEN WE GOT to the hotel, Blake and I walked into our room and the homies went to theirs. I was gone chill with Blake then go to the other room to fuck with ol girl that was in our dressing rooms. Mill had text and told me they were following us to the room. A nigga was still tipsy, so I was still tryna turn the fuck up. I was gonna leave Blake behind because I didn't wanna disrespect her. I wasn't that type of nigga and even though I was single it was etiquette.

BLAKE HEADED into the restroom and was gone for about ten minutes, so I took it upon myself to lay back on the bed and find something on the TV. Moments later she came back, and she was wearing her panties and bra. I looked over her body and instantly my dick got hard. Her shit was nice and tight. She laid down beside me and pulled her phone from her bag.

"You did so good." she said making me look over to her.

"What you didn't think I had it in me?"

"Nooo." she giggled. "I've heard yo music before. You're very talented. It's just my first time seeing you perform live, other than at the club. I love the way you hold the crowd. They really fuck with you."

"Yeah, shit dope. You know a nigga just got out so I'm happy to get the reaction I'm getting."

"What were you in for?"

"Got caught with a strap. Felon with a firearm basically."

"Ohhh. Well you're talented so no one would ever forget about you."

"Even you?" I asked her, and she looked at me with a faint smile.

"I'll never forget about you Baby." she replied and it was something bout the way she said my name. Nah, that wasn't like Baby, Baby, Yung Baby, it sounded like *Baby*. Like I belonged to her.

"Yo ass bet not ma." I told her seriously. I lifted from the bed and the entire time she was watching me.

"I'll be back. I'mma go fuck with these niggas."

"Okay." was all she responded with. I needed to get far away from this girl before I became a simp. Never in my entire career had I had a bitch on the bus with me, at shows with me or in public period. I mean my BM came to a few shows but nothing major. Even my niggas kept asking me did I really like her and each time I wouldn't lie. However, the thoughts of her being a stripper kinda fucked with my head. I didn't have nothing against strippers; it's just that they were set in their ways. They only gave a fuck about a buck. With Blake, I really didn't get that but you never know; shit it's always good in the beginning. I walked out the room and headed next door for the other room. Before I walked out, I made sure to ask baby girl was she hungry and when she said no, it was a green light.

WHEN I WALKED into the room, it was a room full of all kinds of muthafuckas but this was normal. Every city we hit, we knew people and especially women. As soon as I walked in, I spotted ol girl over by the window with her friends. She looked up at me and I could see the excitement in her eyes. Ignoring her, I walked over to the table that held all the liquor. I grabbed a bottle of Henn and went to holla at Bang. He was booed up with Cori which was a trip because Bang wasn't the type of cup caking nigga. I could tell he really liked Cori and where ever they went with this I was happy for my nigga.

"Un, un, where my girl?"

"She in the room."

"Let me find out Baby." she said and pulled out her phone. I knew she was prolly texting Blake but I didn't trip. If she did wanna come it was cool because I didn't plan on doing too much. I hit Cori wit a quick laugh and headed back into the main room to holla at everybody.

WHEN I WALKED IN, everyone was pretty much drinking and socializing. I headed over to ol girl and took a seat near her and her friend. Before I knew it, about an hour had flown by and fucking with Bang it was all jokes. I learned her name was Draylen and her home girl name was Marisha. I made plans to link up with Draylen because she was sexy as fuck with a cool personality. However, the whole time my mind kept wandering to Blake. I was hoping she would come down any minute but she never did so I was gonna chill for a couple more hours then head up to cuddle under her ass.

11

Mic Check 11

BLAKE 'PURE SEDUCTION' BAILEE

I heard the door open and it woke me up out of my sleep. I wasn't a hard sleeper and the excitement of knowing it was Baby wouldn't let me fall into a deep sleep. I laid still in my spot and didn't look over. I didn't want him to think I was on some thirsty shit. Cori had texted me to come up but because he didn't invite me I decided to just chill in the room and watch television. The entire time he was gone, my phone wouldn't stop ringing. Lenox had called telling me he was sorry and Courtney text saying don't come back. When I told her where I was, she said she already knew because it was the talk of the house. I was sure Champagne had ran her mouth.

"BLAKE YOU SLEEP MA?" Baby called out to me.

"I was. What time is it?" I tried to act like I was tired.

"It's 4:19." he replied and I could tell he was buzzed. I rolled over to face him, and he was coming out of his shirt. After, he took off his pants followed by his briefs. *Oh lord.* My pussy started beating like a heartbeat. This nigga didn't care that his dick was rock hard and standing at attention. He began moving around like it was nothing. He then headed into the restroom and turned on the shower. I wanted so bad to join him but I didn't want him to get the wrong impression. So instead I waited until I knew he was inside and I got up to head in. I walked in and he was already soaping up. I took a seat on the toilet, and we began making small talk.

"Why you ain't get in wit a nigga?" he asked as he ran the water over his face to rinse the soap.

"I don't know." I shrugged shyly.

"I ain't gone bite if you don't want me to."

"I took a shower while you were gone."

"Oh aight." he said and continued his shower.

"So what were you guys doing?" I asked to make conversation.

"Shit just drinking and chilling."

"Oh."

"Why you ain't come?"

"I don't know, I guess because I knew your little friend was coming. I didn't want to impose."

"Man, when you're with me ain't no imposing girl. You could have come."

"And you could have invited me."

He stepped out of the water and began drying off. He kept looking over at me with that sexy grin as if he knew I was watching.

"You gon learn Blake Bailee." he said and I frowned puzzled. "You gon learn that when you with a nigga like me it's your world ma. Ain't no invites." he said and wrapped a towel around his waist. I took it as my cue to get up and when I walked past him he grabbed me, spinning me around to face him. "I told you I'm really feeling you. Ain't no invites ma. You with me and it's your world shorty." after that statement I didn't know how to feel. What I did know was, I fell putty in his hands. There was so much fire burning between us, my pussy was soaking.

Before I knew it, he took my bottom lip into his then began sucking on it. *No Kissing Blake. Got dammit no kissing.* I thought but I couldn't help it. I parted my lips and began kissing him like the girls in the movies. We lip locked for what felt like an eternity until he pulled back and pulled my arm so we can head into the room. We climbed into the bed, and he pulled me into his arms. To my surprise he didn't try to touch me. Instead, he kissed me over and over and I swear each time, I was falling in love. His kisses were sensual. They had meaning but what was his intentions? No kissing was a rule and this was the second rule I broke. First, no strings attached was the biggest and now this. No matter how many tricks were cute or had good dick, I was supposed to hold my head high and don't get emotionally attached. Now here it was, this nigga had me breaking rules that I had been accustomed to for years. *But what?* What could a man like baby do with me? And this was when I came back to the reality of things. He had me on a high but I had to sober up. I needed to be rescued but that shit only happened in movies. Therefore, I made up my mind to leave him alone once we got back.

"Why you looking like that ma?"

"Like what?" I looked over to him and my heart fluttered.

"Shit you zoned out on me. You look worried."

"I'm good." I replied but I wasn't. My mind was all over the place. I wanted so bad to ask him who was Mani remembering the call inside of Gucci but I didn't want him to think I was prying.

"Blake look at me." he grabbed my face and made me face him. "Stop tripping baby girl. I know shit seems crazy

75

because it seems crazy to me. I ain't used to no shit like this. I'm really feeling you and it's scary because I don't know where we going with this. I ain't trying to just fuck on you. I want you around for a lifetime if that's possible." he looked me in the eyes. I melted.

"I'll be around but what's gonna happen to us?" I asked ready to tear up. This nigga had me on some emotional shit. He didn't understand my life and the shit I been through. I wish I could tell him, but I knew he would look at me different.

"I don't know ma. We gotta just go with the flow of life. But what I do know is, you ain't going nowhere." he reached over and kissed me once more. I accepted his kiss and laid my head on his chest. I tried so hard not to cry. And the more he rubbed his hands through my hair the more I become impassioned. This man was doing something to me and this is why I had to go.

$$$

WHEN I WALKED into the house I was so nervous but I had to face Lenox. The house was pretty quiet so I was sure everyone was out on a date. I headed for my room to sit my bags down then headed for Lenox's room. I knocked twice and when I heard his voice say come in I hesitated. I walked in, and instantly Lenox and I locked eyes. I dropped my head and walked further in. I took a seat on his bed and the room was silent for a brief moment.

"So how much you make?" Lenox asked in a calm voice. I bent over and reached into my hand bag. I pulled out the money I had gotten from Baby and sat it on the bed. I knew it had to be at least ten grand or so, so I prayed Lenox would accept it and be happy. I looked over at him and his eyes fell from the money back to me.

"Did you fuck him?" he asked in an easy tone.

"No." I turned my head straight so he wouldn't read me.

"Good. " He said and again the room went silent.

"Look, I apologize for putting my hands on you but Pure you know out of all my girls I go easier on you. You've been disrespecting home lately and you know you wrong. When that no good bitch of a mother gave you up, I've been the one loving you and feeding you. Now don't lose your momentum over some rapper nigga. That little nigga got bitches so don't think for one minute he gone wife you up. Don't fuck up your whole life for one night." he said and stood up. "Now go get cleaned up. I need to feel the inside of you and make sure you still pure." he then headed into his restroom. Letting out an exhausting sigh, I stood to my feet and headed to clean up as told.

WHEN I CAME BACK into Lenox room, he was laying in bed naked. I slid into the bed but making sure I grabbed the petroleum jelly. I slid it underneath the pillow then positioned myself so Lenox could climb on top of me. He instantly spread my legs and dived into me from a side angle, so he was in between my legs. His dick wasn't that big, so he was able to slide into me without much moistening. He began pumping me with his short strokes and like always he wrapped his hands inside my hair and tugged at it with each stroke. I hated when he did this because it felt like he was gonna pull my hair out.

"Pure you know...ugh shit, you know who daddy is

baby. I can't let this sweet pussy get away from me." he panted in my ear. "You hear me Blake?"

"Yes daddy."

"It feels good baby?"

"Yes daddy." I lied. I had gotten enough dick in my life to know Lenox dick was the worst on earth. All these years I thought that Courtney was just talking because she hated him but nah, she was serious. Then the whole stick it in thing got to me. It's like right on cue, he screamed out "Stick it in." I slid the jelly from under the pillow and as he continued to stroke me, I greased up my finger.

"Grrrr, stick it in." he whined out not giving me a chance to finish. I reached over around him and when I found his asshole, I slid my finger into it. I began moving it in and out just like he liked it, and he began yelling like a deranged woman. This was the part I hated the most. Just the thought alone always made me wonder was he gay but because I never saw any men or anything out of the norm I figured this was just a part of four play.

"Ohh right there Pureee! Shit right there." he panted again as he fucked my finger. He slid his dick out of me and began stroking it until his nut spilled out. When he fell back onto the bed, my job here was done. I lifted up and instead of going into his restroom I went into mines to wash up.

KNOCK! *Knock!*

THE MOMENT I stepped out of the restroom there was a knock at my door. I knew it was Courtney because I smelled her Obsession perfume seeping underneath. I opened the door and her face frowned. She walked in and took a seat on my bed.

"Why are you back?" she asked with a serious facial expression. I let out a sigh before replying then went on to tell her about my trip with Baby and why I decided to come home.

"So you left because you scared to fall in love with him?"

"No I left because I wasn't about to get my hopes up Court. I really like him and I knew if I stayed around I'd fall silly in love."

"Yeah I feel you but I still think you should have given him a chance. Especially if he didn't try to have sex with you. That should tell you something."

"True but I didn't want to take that chance. And anyway he has a girlfriend."

"Well any chance is better than being here with this nasty finger fucking creep." she said and I burst out into laughter.

"For real bitch. I'm tired of the nigga sex antics. I heard him in there screaming and the first thing that came to mind was somebody in there with they finger in his ass. When I noticed your light on I figured it was you." again I started laughing and this time she joined me on the laugh. "So are you going back to the club?"

"I don't have a choice." I shrugged and in an instant I became sad. Just thinking about going back to dance took away the thoughts of actually getting a job. I wanted to live a normal life and eventually leave Lenox because I knew he wouldn't agree with it. To be truthful he may not let me leave him period. Anytime I mustered up enough energy to ask him I would punk out. I had to figure it out and soon. I was tired of this life and I still had a future ahead of me.

12

Mic Check 12

YUNG BABY

---

2 weeks later

When she on that pole she got a nigga hypnotized.
  She a savage as bitch and she match my fly.
  Private jets, fly her over the city in my G5,
  And every time she cries I just wanna wipe her eyes.
  She my ghetto Cinderella.

"AHHHH." I fucked up for the 5th time and this wasn't like me. I didn't write my music I always just hopped into the booth but for some reason a nigga mind frame wasn't here. Like I said, this wasn't like me. It was always no more than two takes.

Letting out a sigh, I stepped out of the booth and decided to take a shot of something hard. I needed to clear my head. When I walked in, Mill spent around in his chair to look at me. I could tell he was trying to read me and all I could do was shake my head.

"This ain't like you Baby. What's up nigga? Yo head in the clouds."

"Man I'mma get it, I just need to have a drink or something." his eyes fell into slits as he eyed me in silence. "I know you not still bugging over baby girl?"

"Man hell nah nigga. Do you know who the fuck I am? I'm every bitch dream so get the fuck out of here Mill.."

"Yeah, you can pop all that hot shit but you been bugging since she ran out on yo ass. And I'm 99.9 percent sure this song about her. So what we gotta do, get yo little ghetto Cinderella back so you can make music nigga?" he shot making me laugh. He wasn't lying, the song was about Blake.

The day the bus touched down back in Cali she pulled a fast one on a nigga. We were out shopping and out of nowhere she disappeared. I searched damn near every store on Melrose but I couldn't find her nowhere. I went on the bus in hopes she had got back on but there wasn't a trace of her. I picked up the glass Gucci heels she had left behind along with her ID and this is where the song *Ghetto Cinderella* came from. I slid her ID into my pocket but I didn't bother to text her. I figured she ran back to that nigga. A nigga felt played and especially if she went back to ol boy after what he had done to her.

"So the song about that bitch?" Olivia smacked her lips bringing me from a daze. I looked over at her and instantly I got annoyed.

"Why the fuck you worried bout it Liv?"

"I'm just asking." again she smacked her lips.

"Yo why the fuck you here? Yo session ain't until 8." I fumed.

"Oh so now I can't hang around because some stripper hoe got yo panties in a bunch." she stood to her feet.

"Bitch you better watch yo fucking mouth before I forget you a bitch and knock fire from yo ass. You just mad because that stripper hoe getting this dick and yo frail ass can't get it."

"Liv just roll before you piss him off more." Mill jumped up and hopped in between us. He knew once I got started wasn't no stopping. He also knew how I was with Liv. It was strictly business with us. The bitch wanted to fuck me bad and always hated anytime I brought bitches around. That's exactly why I dealt with her with a long handle spoon.

"Yeah bitch roll before you piss me off more." I told her and turned to head back into the booth. I watched her through the glass as she snatched her purse up from the seat and stormed out.

"Run that track back." I told Mill as he continued to shake his head. Right now I ain't give a fuck about Liv feelings. The bitch was dead weight around here anyway. She was good for 1 thing and that was singing hooks. The hoe couldn't even finish her fucking album too busy chasing dick and that was her problem.

20 MINUTES LATER, I finished my track and doubled my ad-libs. Satisfied, I stepped out the booth and jumped behind the sound board so I can mix my own shit. I needed Mill to check emails and set up the next show, which was gonna be another huge one. We were performing at the Staple Center right here in Cali. The first segment of the show was gonna be a huge tribute to Nipsey Hussle. I was still locked up when he got murdered,

so I heard about it in jail. That shit had a nigga sick. I fucked with Nip and YG from time to time and until this day YG was still fucked up. I made it my business to reach out to him every chance I got.

I quickly mix and mastered my track and headed out the door. I needed to see my daughter and hopefully get some pussy from my baby mama. I hadn't had no pussy in a minute so right now Tris was on the list. I could have went to fuck one of my little bitches but I hadn't seen my daughter in weeks.

$$$

"SO WHO'S this new chick you parading around the city with?" Tris asked not even letting me get into the house good enough.

"Man, where my baby?"

"She's sleep. Where you think?" I looked up the hallway in hopes she would run out from her room. I walked over and sat my bag down on the sofa then headed into the kitchen to find some liquor. There was a bottle of Hennessy in the door so I grabbed it and popped it open. I poured me a glass then headed back into the living room where Tris was sitting in front of the TV.

"Aye, turn that up." I told Tris referring to the DJ Khaled video that was playing. I began to bop my head to the track; the shit was hard as fuck. The song was called *You Stay* and I swear I wanted to reach out to that nigga for a remix.

· · ·

UH, I don't know how you do it, but you did it, I'll admit it
And who am I to be a critic and tell you different?
You know I never speak on that nigga, it's not my business
But I could tell you that his level's no competition

I BEGAN RAPPING Meek's part and fell into a zone. The song reminded me of Blake; I'm talking word for word. I could feel Tris eyes on me but I didn't give a fuck. This was a dope ass song and just like Khaled said "Another One." One thing about me, I loved music. I didn't just listen to my own. To be truthful, I got tired of my own music. After hearing it a thousand times in the studio then performing it, I always played other niggas' music. I fucked with Meek heavy, and I was on this new Charlotte rapper named DaBaby. Often in interviews, I would always get asked about name conflict between me, him and Lil Baby but it didn't bother me because Baby was my government name. Lil Baby was another new dope artist that had some hits and especially that *Close Friends*. I liked the song and the video was goals. He had his girl in the video and one day I wished I'd find a bitch I loved enough to throw in a video or two.

"So who is she?" Tris asked making me look over at her.

"Who is who Tris?" I took a sip from my cup.

"The bitch that's been with you. And I know she's been with you because she was with you on stage in Oak then there's a picture of her again with you on Melrose." she began scrolling in her phone and sure enough there were pictures of Blake along with the crew. Wasn't shit intimidating though so Tris was just assuming.

"She ain't nobody. Just came along with the team. Shit Bang might be fucking or Mill might've hit." I brushed her off like it wasn't shit and took a sip from my drank.

"So why are you here?"

"Get some pussy. What's up?" I smirked in her direction, and she had the nerve to shake her head like she wasn't wit it.

"So that's all I am to you is roll through pussy?"

"Man, I came to see my daughter if you wanna be technical. I was just gone try to fuck if you let me. If not I'm not tripping ma."

"What you gone do when you roll through and there's somebody else in yo bed Baby?"

"I ain't gone do shit because that ain't gone happen. You know I'll kill you and any nigga you fucking. Wait, let me reframe that. I don't give a fuck what you do, just don't do it with my baby in here. You got money. You betta go get you a hotel room or some shit."

"Nigga, this my house. And I'm tired of just waiting around on you to come be with us. I'm telling you, nigga, one day I'mma find somebody to love me and you gone be sick."

"I ain't gone be shit. You gone be sick. Get this through your head, baby girl. You can go find any nigga in the world and he ain't gone be me. You'll never get a nigga like me."

"Who said it had to be a nigga?" she smirked. "And nigga you ain't shit."

"Yeah, but you'll sit around for another ten years and wait for my *ain't shit* ass. Look, all I ask is you go get you a regular nigga. Long as he ain't no rapper you good."

"You can't tell me who to fuck with. If I wanna get a rapper, I'mma fuck a rapper." she smirked back and rolled her eyes like the shit she was saying was cute.

"And you gone be the one looking like an industry hoe.

Go right ahead." I took another gulp. She smacked her lips and shoved me with her elbow.

"I can't stand yo ass." she said in a more playful tone.

"Girl, you love me. Come here and hop on this dick." I told her and laid back on the sofa.

13

Mic Check 13

BLAKE 'PURE SEDUCTION' BAILEE

After leaving the stage, I headed to the back for the dressing room. Moments later, Cori came with my money. I was tired as hell and ready to go home. I had yawned at least three times, and I was sober as hell. Lenox had got my job back and tonight was my first night back. Instead of doing any lap dances, I decided to call it a night. Tonight, I made some decent money, so I was good. Some older guy in an expensive suit showered me with money and even slid his business card into my thong. The entire time I was on stage, I was nervous hoping Cori didn't call Baby up here. I really didn't want to be bothered with him, and I guess I was in my feelings because he didn't bother to call or text me. Every day, I checked my phone and not once did he bother reaching out. I mean, I could understand he was probably upset the way I left, but to me he didn't care enough to fight for my love. It's like he just said fuck me.

"You good ma?" Cori asked breaking my train of thoughts. I looked over at her and nodded my head *yes*.

"No you not. You miss him don't you?"

"Nah, I'm good. Shit, he just said fuck me basically."

"What did you expect Blake? You just jetted out on his ass. Bitch, you didn't even give me a heads up." she laughed making me smile.

"I'm sorry friend." I replied and the room fell silent. I got my thoughts together then looked back over at her.

"I've been through so much in my life, Cori. I'm scared to be let down. I want the fairy tale. I'm sure Baby could give me that but then what? He's just some rapper that would eventually break my heart." I told her seriously.

"You don't know because you didn't give him a chance. If anybody knows, I know, he really likes you." she said sounding like Courtney.

"And I'm not." I grabbed my bag ready to head out. I really didn't feel like having this conversation anymore. I had finally gotten over him, so I wanted to erase any memory of him.

WHEN I WALKED OUTSIDE, I pulled out my phone to call an Uber. Cori was right behind me clutching her bags. "Blake, let me take you home. It's too late." she offered as usual. Normally, I would deny her, but I was so tired I didn't feel like waiting. Although it was only midnight, it was still too damn late to be standing outside waiting on a damn ride.

"Okay." I nodded and we headed for her car. We both tossed our bags into the back and climbed in. It's like right on cue, my stomach growled and Cori said at the same time a bitch hungry. I couldn't do shit but laugh then tell her why I was laughing.

"Let's go eat."

"Where? The only thing open is prolly nasty ass Jack in the Box."

"Bitch, we thousand dollar bitches. I ain't eating no damn Jack in the Box." she fussed pulling out her phone.

"Bossa Nova." I suggested and she agreed. The restaurant was right up the street, so she made a U-turn and headed for Sunset Blvd. I couldn't wait to dive into their pasta. I loved *Bossa Nova* and not to mention they stayed open until 4AM. So this was where I went on dates because I wouldn't really be seen by someone I knew.

WALKING TO OUR SEATS, I picked up the menu the moment I sat down. I already knew what I wanted, but I was unsure about my drink. Apparently, Cori knew what she wanted because she told the waiter we were ready to order. After putting in our order we began to make small talk until I felt my pee sitting on my bladder. I jumped up from the table and ran into the restroom and right into the empty stall. I heard the sound of the toilet flushing next to me, so I knew I wasn't here alone. After I was done, I headed out to wash my hands and there was a lady standing there in a two piece jean suit.

"Excuse me." I told her reaching over to grab a paper towel. She was applying her lip gloss until she stopped to look at me. I watched her reflection in the mirror, and she was eyeing me like she knew me.

"Umm, do I know you from somewhere?" she asked.

"I don't know. Ummm, did you go to Audubon Middle School?"

"No. I didn't grow up out here. I'm from New York."

"I guess there's no telling then. I work at Crazy Girlz. Maybe you've seen me there."

"The strip club?"

"Yes."

"Oh okay." she replied and without another word she headed out the restroom.

Walking out behind the chick, I headed for our table. I saw the same chick taking a seat at a table next to a little girl. She said something to the guy that was with her, but I couldn't hear nor tell who it was. Whatever she said, it had to be about me because she looked over in my direction and shortly after, Baby and I locked eyes. I stood frozen for a moment, then I quickly snapped back and ran over to the table. I slid into the booth and Cori was looking at me weird.

"Why you looking like that?" she asked, but I was too embarrassed to tell her. I was in shame because I had told Baby's girl I was a damn stripper.

"Girl, Baby over there with Mani." I dropped my head.

"Mani?"

"His girl. I heard him talking to her on the..." before I could finish, Cori signaled me, so I knew he was behind me.

"Sup sis, what's up Blake?" his voice danced off the back of my neck. He then stepped in front of me and I replied *Hey* like I wasn't moved by his presence.

"That's all a nigga get is a hey?"

"What I'm supposed to say Baby?"

"Shit, you can start by explaining why you just shake a nigga with not as much as a bye."

"I don't owe you an explanation. We're not together." I snarled. I was still salty about seeing him with his chick so right now I didn't feel like I needed to explain myself.

"Oh word?" he threw his head back and began rubbing his chin.

"I'm ready." we turned to the voice that had walked up.

It was the same chick from the restroom, and she was holding the little girl that was now sleep in her arms.

"Aight." he said and looked back to me. When I turned my head, he let out a chuckle then told Cori he'd holler at her. Baby walked out with the girl in tow and I let out a sigh that I had been holding for some time. Cori looked at me, but she didn't say a word.

"I guess the nigga do got a girl." she replied as if she was waiting on me to say told you so but I didn't. I knew if I sparked it up we would go on and on and the way I was feeling, I really didn't wanna be bothered with the conversation of Baby. Instead, I asked her about Bang and when I mentioned his name, her eyes lit up. Damn, I remember having that same spark in my eyes weeks ago. I was happy for my girl but I'd be lying if I said I wasn't a bit jealous.

BY THE TIME I got home it was almost 3 in the morning. I knew Lenox was probably up because the front light was on. When I walked in, instead of seeing Lenox, Champagne and her normal trick were seated inside the dining area. I walked past them happy as hell it wasn't Lenox. I went into my room and prepared myself for my shower. I was glad I didn't dance on Sundays, so I can spend the day lying around. The sound of my text dinged and a shock wave went through my body thinking it may have been Baby. I quickly pulled it from my bag and when I read the text it was Cori.

CORI: *don't be stressing and shit over that nigga friend.*
    Me: *LOL OMG* 😂 *Girl I'm not. Baby is the last thing on my mind.*

. . .

91

I LIED.

CORI: *okay well you have a good night. Call me tomorrow.*
I'm going to chill with Bang so you know I'mma have an earful for you 😔

Me: *LOL okay. Good night friend* 🌙 😔

14

Mic Check 14

YUNG BABY

The next morning, I woke up with Blake heavy on my mind. Seeing her with Cori told me her ass went back to that damn club after I asked her not to. Shit had me low key hot because I gave her a few stacks to hold her over until I gave her more. Now I know y'all might hear this all the time but it's real shit. I ain't no trick. I really like Blake and to keep her safe and away from that club I'd do anything for her.

Last night her little ass got slick at the mouth. Knowing about the club and that slick ass comment, I wanted to yoke her ass up. I knew she was prolly tripping because she saw me with Tris but it wasn't like that. I had told Tris not to cook. I was gonna bring them something to eat but I got caught up in the studio all day. Therefore, I decided to just take them to Bossa Nova to grab something quick. I hated Tris had to see her because whatever words they exchanged in the restroom, she couldn't wait to come back to the table and brag about seeing my *stripper hoe* in the bathroom. I brushed her ass off because she didn't drop a name, but when Blake emerged from the restroom a nigga emotions shifted. I was happy to see her but still caught up over the way she just shook a nigga. So right now here I was ready to finally be the one to break the ice. I pulled out my phone and began texting her.

ME: *a nigga miss the fuck outta of you*

I SAT my phone down in hopes she would reply. A few minutes went by and when I heard my alert I eagerly picked it up.

BLAKE: *How is that when you got a girl?* 😏
  Me: *That's my daughter mother and it ain't even like that.*
  All we did was go grab something to eat.

I SAT THERE for a few minutes just listening to a track. When she didn't respond I dialed her number because she had me fucked up. I swear after this I was gonna give up on Blake.

"HELLO." she whispered into the phone and I instantly got hot.

"What's up, you with that nigga or something?" there was a faint pause before she replied. I could tell she was walking because I could hear the phone moving around.

"No, I'm not with nobody." her ass was lying right through her teeth.

"So why the fuck you whispering ma?" I shook my head as if she could see me. "Blake I miss yo ass. That was fucked up how you did me shorty. I thought we were on to something."

"We were Baby." she let out a soft sigh. "It's just… It's just… you have to understand that…" before she could finish the sound of a muscular voice could be heard in the background.

"Who the fuck you sneaking around on the phone with bitch!" his voice boomed loudly through the phone.

"I'm not on the phone." I could hear the frantic in her voice.

"Bitch, you a muthafucking lie!" he roared and I know I wasn't tripping; it sounded like he slapped her. The sound of Blake's scream echoed through the phone and I could tell he began to attack her. Shortly after I could hear a female voice in the background.

"Oh my god, you gonna kill her! Please stop!" I could tell the chick was crying. My blood instantly boiled and that's when it clicked. I still had Blake's ID that I had put into my glove box. Disconnecting the phone I ran out the studio and hopped into my whip. I pulled the ID from the glove box and punched the address into my GPS. It said I would be there in 28 minutes. I just prayed I'd make it before the nigga killed her.

I WAS to the address in record time and just as I pulled up, Mill, Bang and Tay were pulling up at the same time. I had called them niggas while I was on the way and it's like God was on Blake side because they were at Barkley's on Labrea getting food. I grabbed my strap from under my seat and tucked into my waist. I jumped out the car and my boys followed suit. We headed up to the door and Bang used his gun to bam on the door. Shortly after a female came to the door.

"Baby." she said my name in a panic as she unlocked the door.

"Where she at?"

"She's in the back, and she fucked up." she said as tears poured from her eyes. I rushed to the back with my goons right behind me and each door I passed by I stuck my head inside. When I reached the room Blake was in, she was laid out on the ground, and she appeared to be unconscious.

"Take her to the whip Tay."

Tay ran over to her body. When I stepped further into the room, the same guy that had beat her ass at the club was sitting in a chair like nothing ever happened. I lost it. I ran over to where he sat and started punching the nigga so hard the side of his bones cracking echoed through the room. Mill and Bang followed suit and next thing I know we had beat the nigga until he was unconscious. I swear I wanted to kill him but because three other girls had run into the room I decided not to. I knew if I killed him I would have to kill them and right now a nigga ain't have time for no cleanups.

"It's your 2nd lucky day bitch! 3 times you strike out." I kicked ol boy one last time then motioned for my crew.

We ran up out the house and hopped into the whips. I sped off and headed for Southern California Hospital. Each light I stopped at, I looked back at Blake. The side of her head was covered with blood, and she was still out of it. The more I looked at her the more I wanted to kill that nigga. A part of me felt like this shit was all my fault, but fuck that, Blake is fragile as fuck. Too fragile for some grown ass man to be putting his hands on her. It seemed like this shit was regular to this nigga. And another part seemed like Blake liked the shit. I swear after this go round if she decided to go back, I was gonna cut her completely short. There was no way I could fuck with a weak bitch. I mean, I know I had to figure things out with her, but she had to give me a chance. And that was Blake's problem; she wouldn't give a nigga a chance.

WHEN WE PULLED into the hospital, I quickly jumped out and pulled Blake into my arms. I ran into the hospital and right up to the front desk. The nurse wide-eyed me and I knew what she was thinking, but when she looked down at Blake her face softened. She rushed over to get a gurney then rushed her to the back immediately. I knew I was gone be here all night, so I told my niggas they could roll. Once I chopped it up with them for a few minutes, I headed into the waiting room and took a seat.

"Yung Baby?" I heard my name being called so I turned towards the door. It was the same nurse who had helped me when I first came in. She motioned for me with her finger, so I stood to my feet and headed towards her. "Were gonna put you in a more private room." she said and told me to follow her. Man I swear this was good looking out. I really didn't want to be in the main room because I ain't feel like being bothered with autographs and shit. My only concern right now was Blake and the way shorty was looking I was praying she wasn't dead.

$$$

"HELLO, I'm Doctor Hampton and you are?"

"Baby Taylor."

"Thank you, Mr. Taylor." he nodded his head. "By any chance can you explain what happened to her?"

"She has to explain that you. All I can tell you is I found her on a sidewalk unconscious."

"Okay." he replied and pulled the clipboard from under his arm. "So far she's doing great. She has about a 3-inch gash on the side of her head where she was stricken pretty hard. The gash is pretty deep but not enough to require stitches. Also, she has a fractured rib. Nothing to worry about because it heals itself. Now if you're gonna be with her after this, I suggest pain pills to help the pain so she could breathe better. I'll be prescribing her some acetaminophen now for pain. Just make sure she doesn't put on anything tight. In about a month or so, she should be fine. She's under medication right now but she'll be awake soon. You can head up to see her. The nurse will give you a pass and the room information. Once again, I'm Dr. Hampton; if you have any questions have the nurse page me."

"Thanks Doc."

I shook his hand and headed for the nurses' station. Once I got the pass I headed upstairs. When I walked into her room, she was laying in the bed peacefully. Her lip was kind of swollen, and she had a patch on her head where the gash was. Other than that, her injuries were pretty much internal. I walked over to the chair and took a seat. I was gonna be here when she opened her eyes. I had so much work to do but right now none of that shit mattered. Like I said before, I had to make sure shorty was straight.

15

Mic Check 15

BLAKE BAILEE

When I opened my eyes, my head was slightly spinning. I had to focus in on where I was because I didn't remember anything. When I noticed the happy face on that wall the symbolized pain, I knew I was in the hospital. Everything that transpired began to play in my mind and my thoughts were vivid as to what happened. I remembered talking to Baby on the phone and Lenox crept up on me out of nowhere. The nigga didn't even bother checking my phone. Instead, he assumed and next thing I know he began beating the shit out of me until I passed out. The sound of Courtney cries was the last thing I heard before I blanked out.

"Sup ma?" I turned towards the voice and Baby was sitting in the chair right beside the bed.

"Hey." I replied embarrassed wondering how the hell he ended up here.

"How you feel?" he asked standing up from his seat. He walked over to the bed and leaned on the rails.

"I'm okay, I guess. Thank you for coming." I faintly smiled. I began twirling my fingers then mustered up enough courage to ask him. "How you did you know I was here?"

"Shit, I stayed on the phone when ol boy came in. I heard everything. And if you're wondering how I found you, you left your ID on the bus. Shit, I went to the address that was on there."

"Oh...ummm, so what happened?" I asked wondering what happened with him and Lenox.

"Shit, I beat the nigga ass. Left him the same way he left you."

"Oh my god, you didn't kill him, did you?" I asked scared. Before I could continue, Baby hit me with a disturbed look.

"After the shit he did to you, you're worried bout him?" he frowned.

"Fuck him. I just don't want anything to happen to you Baby."

"I'm straight ma. After what he did to you, he'd be a bold muthafucka to go to the police." I nodded my head in agreeance.

"Look, I know you wondering what happened to me that day and what's going on in my life. It's pretty complicated but I will tell you this. Some things happened when I was younger, and I was sent to live with Lenox. I didn't have anyone all my life so once I met you I actually started falling for you; and fast. The night in the hotel after we talked, I made up my mind and decided to go back home. It wasn't nothing you did; it was me. I really didn't know where we were going and I didn't want to risk losing everything for just a quick fling. I know you have a girl and that's another thing. Not to mention, the many women that comes with your lifestyle. This is Hollywood Baby. I'm not in a position to compete with these bitches." I looked over at him and tears began to pour from my eyes. He reached over and wiped my tears then looked me in the eyes.

"Blake, let's get this straight...I don't have a girl. And real shit, I get what you saying about my lifestyle but really this shit ain't what you think. True, I got mad bitches but since I met you all I've been focused on was you. Can't no bitch stand next you so get that competition shit out yo head. A nigga getting older and I can't believe I'm bout to say this but I wouldn't mind giving us a shot."

"Are you serious?" I asked wiping my own tears. Just hearing him mention giving us a shot gave me hope. After this, I didn't want to go back to Lenox. If I had to sleep on a park bench then so be it but I wasn't going back.

"Hell yeah, I'm serious." he smiled exposing his deep dimple. When he licked his lips, I melted. "Only on two conditions." he said and his face got serious. "You can't go back to that nigga or that club. You belong to me now so you don't need shit from here on out. Deal?" he said and lifted his pinky for me to swear along with him.

"Deal."

I smiled and again he hit me with that sexy ass dimple. When the room went silent, I dropped my head. Baby lifted my chin and made me face him. He then reached over to kiss me and again I melted. Although I was physically abused, I was emotionally happy right now. I didn't know what it would be like to be a rapper's girlfriend, but I guess if he was willing to give us a try, I would soon find out. I wanted to ask him about where would I be living but I just relished at the moment. He said he had me, so I guess he had me.

$$$

One month later

Ever since I left the hospital I've been by Baby's side. He eased my curiosity by moving me into his mansion. The home was so beautiful, I fell in love the moment we pulled into the driveway. He looked over and smirked at me with a *"welcome home baby."* and ever since then I felt like I had been living that fairy tale I always dreamed about.

Baby was everything a woman could ask for in a man. Although he was cocky as hell, when it came to me he was putty. He treated me like a queen and, trip this, we hadn't had sex yet. I was still slightly healing, but I was able to move around better. He hired me an in-home nurse and because he already had a maid I didn't have to lift a finger.

Days he would go to the studio, he would call me every hour. I don't know if he was worried about me or was he scared I would leave again but the nigga called constantly. I assured him over and over I wasn't going anywhere and each time he would make me promise. I actually found it kind of cute.

This man was doing something to me and fast. I would lie around in the bed missing him each time he left and, when he would walk in, I would light up like a Christmas tree on December 24th. Tonight, I had something planned for him. Since I was feeling much better, I decided to get up, shower and head outside to take a swim. Before I headed out, I pulled out my phone so I could call Cori. I dialed her number and waited for her to answer.

"Hey ma?" her voice graced the phone.

"Heyy. What you doing?"

"Girl shit, about to take these niggas some food to the studio."

"Good, and if some girls up there you better tell me."

"Oh my god girl." she burst out laughing. "That man ain't doing shit but working. You know Baby, *no distractions* as he calls it. Bitch, I didn't tell you I almost had to beat that bitch Olivia Luv up."

"What!? What happened?"

"Girl, the bitch just got a slick ass mouth. When I hopped up in her face, Mill broke us up. Baby told me he almost had to beat her ass recently, too, but I told him don't worry; that's what I'm here for." she boasted, and we both laughed.

"I do not like her."

"Me either. But fuck that hoe. What you doing?"

"Girl home bored. I need a favor though."

"Anything for you my love."

"I need some candles and something sexy to wear."

"To do what in Blake?"

"Nothing like that." I laughed. "I just wanna get sexy for him tonight. Maybe I can finally get some."

"Bitch, you still ain't gave that man none?"

"No." I laughed shaking my head.

"Okay, I'll slide through Hollywood Blvd to one of those lingerie shops. What color?"

"Umm, red."

"No red, you'll look like a prostitute. How about baby blue." she added but her statement rubbed me wrong.

"Hello."

"Yes, I'm here. Umm, baby blue is fine."

"Okay, well give me about an hour."

"Okay, thanks friend."

"You're welcome baby, see you soon." we disconnected the line.

I headed out the room and out the door for the pool. When I stepped out. I was met with the bright sun. It had to be at least 100 degrees because it was hot as hell. Inside the house was always so cool so I wasn't prepared for the heat. I quickly took off my robe and took the stairs down slowly into the pool. The water was lukewarm, so I eased right on in. I don't know if I was supposed to move around much but I didn't wanna handicap myself so I swam a few laps. The entire time I thought of tonight. I couldn't wait to surprise Baby. I was so damn ready to take that next step before his ass decided to step out. I was gonna give him a taste of my world-famous head and try my best to put this pussy on him. I knew he would be surprised, and although I was nervous I was eager as hell.

16

Mic Check 16

YUNG BABY

I was driving down PCH listening to my new track I just laid. The shit was dope as hell, so I bopped my head to the beat like it wasn't mines. I listened to it good trying to figure out a dope hook. Mill thought Liv would be dope on the track and even though I was still salty with her I agreed. The sound of my phone rang through the Bluetooth and seeing that it was a collect call I answered.

"You have a collect call from Royal Kane." I quickly hit 5 to accept the call.

"Sup nigga?"

"Baby. What's da deal nigga?"

"Shit, just rolling. How you doing my nigga?"

"Shit, I'm straight. Just taking this shit one day at a time." he said but I could tell he was stressed out. Anytime I talked to Kane, he had me feeling fucked up. He was currently doing time for murder on a producer named Richy Rich. Shit was crazy because I was cool with both them niggas. I had copped plenty tracks for Rich and had for years. He had signed Kane to his label and that's how I met him. Kane was a cool ass nigga with a savage ass attitude. He reminded me of myself in a sense. Some shit had happened between them over a chick name Lyric A who was a stylist. Make a long story short, she was Kane's girl and started fucking with Rich. The two of them started beefing and shit got wild. They started making diss tracks first then next thing you know bullets began flying.

First, Kane got popped then he retaliated by killing Rich. In the process, he even popped Lyric A. Nigga got washed up for the murder, but he was doing good because Lyric A had been by his side riding it out with him. An author by the name of Barbie Scott wrote a book about those niggas lives called *A Boss Got Me In My Feelings But A Savage Got My Heart*. I actually read the book while I was locked up; shit was dope.

"You need anything?" I asked knowing he was straight. That nigga was a young millionaire and Lyric A had bread, too, but it was etiquette that I ask my nigga.

"Nah, I'm good foo. Good looking."

"Always."

KANE and I continued to chop it up for the short 15 minute call he had. By the time we ended the call, I was pulling up to my crib. I pulled into my driveway and grabbed the bags of food then climbed out. When I headed into the house, I figured Jana was in the room and Blake had to be sleep. The house was pitch dark and it was only a little after 9PM. I sat the food down on the counter top and headed for my bedroom anxiously. A nigga had missed Blake all day, and I couldn't wait to get home. Ever since she's been living in my crib, I merely wanted to leave the house. When I was in the studio working she would cross my mind every so often. I don't know what this chick was doing to me, but she had a nigga bugging.

WHEN I GOT to my bedroom door, it was closed but I could see the flicker of a light from underneath. Pushing the door open, I got the shock of my life. There were candles lit throughout the room and Blake laid on the bed in a two piece silk lingerie set.

"*Damn,*" escaped my lips because the flicker of the candle light danced off her body making her look exotic. The way she was laying, exposed the curve in her hip making my dick instantly hard. Her big bedroom eyes looked up at me and when she bit into her bottom lip I walked further into the room impatiently. I swear she didn't have to tell me twice. I stepped out of my shoes followed by my pants. I then peeled out of my wife beater but I made sure to leave my chains on. I removed my *LA* cap and placed it on the dresser then climbed into the bed next to her.

"KEEP DOING shit like this and I ain't gone never leave the crib." I pulled at her arm so she could slide all the way to my side of the bed.

"Oh yeah?" she asked and tossed her leg over me.

"You must be ready for me to punish that pussy."

"I been ready." she replied seductively.

She reached over and grabbed a hand full of my dick, so I pulled my briefs off. When she lifted onto her knees and moved down to my dick it fucked me up because I didn't expect her to...*oh yeah, she did it*. I thought as Blake took my dick into her hand and began teasing it with her tongue. I rested my hands behind my head ready to see what she had. Not even a minute later, she had a nigga eyes widened and my toes damn near curling. I swear I wasn't expecting this shit. This girl had my whole dick down her throat and hadn't gagged once. She began moving up and down covering my dick in spit.

"Fuck ma, fuck you learn this shit at?" I asked biting into my lip. I mean, I know she was a dancer but this shit didn't have shit to do with dancing.

Her eyes found mines, but she didn't stop sucking. She had a nigga squirming, jumping and ready to scream like hoe. Therefore, she had me fucked up. I wasn't ready to bust, so I motioned for her to stop and bend that ass over. When she lifted her head up she wiped the spit from her mouth and a huge smirk crept up on her face.

"Yeah, I got something for yo ass. I hope that stomach healed because you got me messed up Blake Bailee." I told her and positioned myself behind her. Since my dick was soaking wet I spread her ass open and slid inside of her slowly.

"Ahhhhhh!" she let out a deep growl like I was killing her. I didn't know if it was because all this dick I was blessed with or was it because her injury. I continued to go slow then bent down to place kisses on her neck. She threw her head back so I could kiss into the nape of her neck. She then turned her head so I began kissing her lips without missing a stroke.

"Oh my god, Baby ,it feels sooo good." she cried out. I continued to hit that same spot since she said it felt good. My dick filled her insides, and I could feel her muscles locking down on my dick. Ready to hit my famous move, I pushed the top of her all the way down and helped her lift her ass. I lifted up on my feet then used my body to push up inside of her. I made sure to rub my dick across her G Spot and I continued to hit it for a few minutes. The way she began to scream told me I had her where I wanted her.

"Baby, I gotta pee...oh my god, I gotta pee!" she was trying to move but I had her locked in.

"Don't move." I told her and within seconds her pussy gushed out the water fucking up my whole bed. I slid out of her because a nigga couldn't fuck in that shit.

"What was that?" she asked breathing hard.

"You squirted ma."

"Squirt?"

"Yeah, you don't know what squirt is?"

"Yes, I know what it is but I never did it before."

"Trust me, it's a lot of shit you ain't seen but I got this. Now come here." I lifted off the bed and pulled Blake towards the dresser. I told her to have a seat, and she still looked out of it.

WHEN SHE SAT on top of my dresser, I walked right into her pussy and slid my dick back in. Before I got to hitting her with my strokes, I needed to mind fuck her for a minute. I began massaging her clit with my two middle fingers as I watched her. She was watching me with a frown on her face. It wasn't like a painful frown, more like a blissful one. Her head was cocked to the side, and she had this look on her face like *what are you doing to me?*

"Give me kiss." I demanded and waited for her to bring her lips to me. Doing as told, she began kissing me hungrily, but she stopped in between the moan. Finally, I began stroking her pussy but never breaking our kiss. "Blake, this shit mines forever."

"You can have it daddy. Ohhh shit, you can have it allll-ll." That was all I needed to hear. I began fucking her harder to make sure she would remember our first time.

109

We ended up fucking basically all around *our* bedroom. We went at it for hours and I didn't see myself stopping anytime soon. I had a point to prove and this was my chance. Blake Bailee wasn't going nowhere and after this, she was stuck forever. What the hoes say? Period.

17

Mic Check 17

BLAKE BAILEE

"We ain't gone be here that long. I just need Liv to finish this hook, and we can go out to eat."

"Ugh."

"Man don't start."

"Whaaa, I don't like her."

"Shit me either. But fuck that bitch."

"She wants to fuck you. I could tell."

"Shit what bitch don't?" Baby looked over at me with a smirk.

"Get them hoes fucked up." I told him seriously. I wasn't playing with Baby and these bitches. I swear since the other night when we fucked, this nigga had me all dumb over him. I was five seconds from telling him I loved him but I caught myself.

"Since a nigga made that pussy squirt you sure been tripping ma." he looked over from the driver side. *Damn it's that obvious?* I thought to myself with my head trained in the opposite direction from him. I was so damn embarrassed I couldn't face him. "It's aight baby. Shit kinda cute. It shows me you care.

"I do care." I spoke just above a whisper.

"That's what's up." he replied and sped off gassing his engine. He turned the music up and the same song he always played boomed through his speakers. He played the song so much I was beginning to think he was trying to send me a message. For some reason he rapped Meek Mills part the most. Instead of asking him, I just bopped my head and let the words sink in.

WHEN WE PULLED up to the studio I noticed Cori's car out front, and I was happy as hell. I also noticed many other cars so I knew the inside was packed. This was my first time seeing everyone since Oakland so I was a bit nervous. Everyone knew that Baby and I were now an item because they would always call for him when he was working and ask if I was hungry or to let me know he was in the booth and would be leaving soon. Because Bang and Cori were cozy with each other me and him would always hold conversations. Mill was cool but he was more business savvy. He kept it brief and short.

WHEN WE WALKED IN, I was hit with a cloud of smoke. It was so crowded I could barely see inside. However, the smell of Victoria's Secret spray mixed throughout the air and the sounds of chattering filled the air. When we stepped fully inside there was barely anywhere to sit. Olivia was sitting on the sofa with two other chicks, Bang and Cori were sitting on the other love seat, Mill was at the soundboards and a few other guys stood around.

"Blakeyyy!" Cori cooed my name then made Bang get up so I could sit down. When I walked over to her, I could feel Olivia's eyes glued to me along with her friends. I ignored them and took a seat next to my friend.

"Them bitches got a fucking staring problem." Cori leaned over and whispered in my ear. I looked over in their direction, and they were all watching me but one. Her eyes were trained on Baby, but he paid her no mind.

"Damn, what's up Baby. You can't speak?" she said with a slight neck roll.

"Sup Patience." he replied dryly. As rude as Baby was I was surprised he didn't say some slick shit. And because he didn't this had my antennas up. I wondered if he actually fucked her instead of Liv. Or maybe because he was fucking Liv her friend felt like he was obligated to be cool with her. Whatever the case was, he was fucking one of them bitches.

"Here Blake." I looked up and Bang was handing me a cup. I reluctantly took it because I was still taking my meds but since I hadn't taken one in the last four hours I decided to drink it. Getting comfy, Cori and I began gossiping while the fellas worked. Baby walked into the booth and began his music and from time to time I would look over at him. He looked so damn sexy behind the glass with his headphones on. Each time he rapped, his iced out grill beamed against the glass. His energy was so dope to me. He was very animated while he recorded just how he was when he performed. He really didn't dance, but he had this one dumb dance he did that the crowd loved. It was so funny to me, but he looked cute doing it.

WHEN I TURNED to look towards the giggling, the same chick was eyeing Baby and the rest of them were bopping to his song. When he stepped from inside the booth he and I locked eyes and I slightly rolled my neck. My eyes shifted towards the chick and when he looked over it told him why I was tripping. He took a seat in the spin chair and spent around to look at me.

"Blake come here." he told me and I tried to act like I didn't want to jump. I took my sweet time and when I walked over to him he chuckled and pulled me down to his lap.

"Liv you up." Mill spent in his chair. She stood from her seat and walked into the booth. She slid on the headphones and Mill dropped the beat. She began to bop her head and once the beat dropped for her part she began singing the hook. I don't know if it was me, but she was off-key.

"You off." Mill spoke into the mic. She nodded her head and the beat came on again. Before I knew it, she had done the song at least thirty times and each time she was off. I could tell she was beginning to get frustrated. She stepped from inside the booth and said she needed a drink.

"Maybe that's the problem, yo ass drunk." Baby said embarrassing her. When everyone laughed, I kinda felt bad for her.

"She sounded good, just a little off. You did good though." I told her and to my surprise she smiled.

"Thanks." she replied.

"I'M HIS GHETTO CINDERELLA, rainy days umbrellas.
Gucci shades when we together,
We pack Ninas and Berettas.
Baby down for whatever, and I'll neva let you goooo
We gone be together and let the whole world knowww."

"JUST RIDE THE BEAT." I told her and I could feel all eyes

114

on me. I knew I was drunk because the only time I sung was in the privacy of a shower.

"Damn yo, that shit sounded good." Mill said, and he was still bopping his head as if I was still singing.

"Hell yeah Blake."

"Ayo get in the booth and run that back just like you did." Mill told me. I looked around the room and now Liv had a slight frown. I wasn't trying to steal her shine. I just wanted to help. Because the pressure was on me, I got up and headed inside. Mill played the track back and just like that I began singing my heart out. The song was dope as hell.

"Like that?" I asked unsure when I heard Mill stop the track. He spun in his chair and faced Baby.

"Man what you wanna do because baby girl sound good as hell?"

"Shit, let's keep her on there." Baby said and looked at me.

"So y'all replacing me with her?" Olivia voiced.

"Man Liv chill. You on a million songs and this one just ain't for you."

"I'm just faded right now." she tried to reason.

"Next one." Mill said dismissing her. She smacked her lips and sat back. I took my seat on Baby's lap and I felt horrible. I mean, I was happy as hell I was on the song but I couldn't rub it in.

"Where you learn to sing like that ma?"

"I was lead in my church choir growing up."

"Word? And why you ain't never tell me you could sing like that?" he asked and I shrugged my shoulders. The music played in the background and I could tell Baby was feeling it. Bang and Cori were in tune with it and of course Mill loved it because he kept shouting and shit making some crazy noises.

"Yung Baby featuring Blake Bailee!" Mill shouted excited. He started the track over and began mixing it.

"My baby on a track with me." Baby rubbed my back as he smiled into my neck making me giggle. I swear this shit was like a dream come true. Since I was a little girl I always dreamed of being a R&B singer. Who would have ever thought I would be on a song with thee Yung Baby. Now, I didn't wanna jump to conclusions because he may have used Liv for the video which would be dumb because we sounded totally different. But I couldn't tell him how to run his business so I would let him do him. All I know is, I did a track with Yung Baby and I would forever be grateful.

18

Mic Check 18

OLIVIA LUV

I sat back on the sofa with my arms folded over my chest and a pout on my face. Everything my girls were saying went through one ear and out the other. Their constant giggling was annoying the fuck out of my soul because I was sitting over here going through some shit. My feelings were so fucking hurt right now, I didn't find shit funny nor cared about anything they were saying. My heart was beating in my chest and looking over at Baby he wasn't making matters any better. Already he had shitted on me by not giving me a chance and now he let this bitch take a song from me that I was actually hyped over.

To make matters worse, he did the shit in front of everybody. Bang was laughing, and his little stripper bitch was gassing Blake up. Then here was Baby, the man that I was head over heels in love with, not making the situation any better. I didn't understand what the fuck he seen in her that he didn't see in me. The bitch was a hoe in my eyes, and he wifed the bitch. I have done everything in my power to get Baby but the nigga never budged. He hit me with some, 'he doesn't mix business with pleasure' bullshit that knocked my confidence level down. I wanted this man, whether he fucked my friend or not. I wanted him first and the bitch knew that so I didn't care if she found out, I would still fuck him.

For so long I didn't fuck with Patience because she knew how I felt about him and took upon herself to still throw him the pussy. The only reason we were cool now is because he fucked her and dissed her. He completely shitted on her little dreams of having a rapper as a boyfriend.

WHEN I FIRST MET BABY, I had met him through Tay. We were at a club and I did everything to get Baby to notice me without looking thirsty but the shit didn't work. He ignored my ass, and that's when Tay noticed me. We began hitting it off but because I was so in love with Baby I didn't play too much into it. We exchanged numbers and shortly after I came to the studio. Baby had ended up going to jail before I got the chance to meet him, but after singing for Tay and Mill I was signed. I became part of BBE and I did everything to get on everyone's good side. I even went to visit Baby while he was locked up. I was hoping to make him fall for me and see I was a down chick but each visit was strictly artist and CEO. The nigga just wouldn't fuck with me.

Now here it was, a bitch who degraded herself for a living had this nigga wrapped around her finger. And I swear since the day she came into the picture he had been acting funny. I mean, Baby and I weren't the best of friends, but we were a team. Now he was acting like anytime I was around I was annoying him, and he barely said two words to me. The last time he blew up on me wasn't because of what I said, it was because this nigga was in his feelings over the bitch just leaving him. The way he spoke to me that day, crushed the little of heart I did have. This nigga made me wanna just stay away for a while and hope they'll miss me. But when I got the call that I was needed for the Cinderella hook, I was ecstatic. I knew this was my chance to get back in his good graces, but nope, once again my little parade was stormed on.

I WATCHED Baby as he stood up along with his little bitch. I could tell he was about to leave and instantly I became sad. I was so gone off this nigga that I didn't give a fuck if he hated me, as long as he was in my presence. And I made it my business to always look good while he was. When he grabbed Blake's hand, I rolled my eyes out of jealousy and trained my attention on something else. When I looked back up, I caught the back of Baby just in time to see him smack her on the ass. Again I rolled my eyes and this time, her friend saw me. She began grilling the fuck out of me and I grilled her ass right back.

"You sure got an eye rolling problem. Yo ass wasn't doing none of this shit while she was just here." she shot at me.

"What the fuck are you talking about?" I rolled my shit at her too.

I was waiting on Mill to speak up but the nigga was acting like he ain't hear what was going on. When she stood up, she walked over by the couch and looked down at me like I was supposed to be scared. I ain't gone lie, the bitch was intimidating as fuck but I couldn't punk out in front of my girls and my team. I stood up and got in her face.

"You got a problem?" I asked her matching her stare. Before I knew it, she hauled off and punched me so hard I flew back into the table. The few bottles of liquor hit the ground and everyone basically sat there.

"Bitch!" I charged at her but I wasn't quick enough. She hit me with an uppercut that nearly dazed me but I couldn't fold. I charged her again and this time I knocked her back into the wall. What the fuck did I do that for? She snatched me down by my hair and pinned me down on the ground. At this point I was waiting for one of these bitches to jump in, but they never did. However, I heard Justine voice yelling let her up.

"Bitch you want some too?" she screamed sounding like Deebo. I tried to use this as my chance to flip her off me but I failed. The bitch began punching me so hard it felt like my face was being bust in.

"Get her off me!" I began screaming out. When I felt her body jerk off me, I knew someone had snatched her off of me.

"Come on y'all, y'all can't be tearing the studio up." Tay was standing over me. I stood to my feet and began running my hands through my hair and my shit was shedding bad. I swear it felt like this hoe pulled my scalp off.

"Yeah bitch, keep popping off at the mouth and this gone always happen." she said as she walked back over to the couch and took a seat like nothing ever happened. I don't know who this bitch was, but I wished she went back where ever the fuck she came from. I was so mad and for the third time tonight I was embarrassed as hell. I snatched my shit up off the couch and stormed out of the studio for my car. I didn't bother to say shit to them bitches and they better find a ride home the best way they could.

Pulling out of the parking lot my hands were shaking and my head was spinning. I was having so many evil thoughts I had to get myself together. I swear I was gonna make both them bitches life a living hell and when I did they would regret fucking with me.

WHEN I FINALLY GOT MYSELF together, I picked up my phone and placed a call. I waited for her to answer and when she did, I broke down crying.

"I can't understand you, what's wrong?"

"This bitch attacked me."

"Who attacked you?"

"That bitch Cori. She rushed me while I wasn't looking." I lied.

"So where was Baby?"

"He's gon with his little bitch. It started all over her hoe ass."

"Wow, so he's gone with her and you up there fighting and shit. That's crazy. Where you at now?"

"I just left. Are you home?"

"Yeah I'm here."

"Okay I'm about to come over."

"Okay, well you know you gotta be gone by the morning in case my baby daddy come."

"Okay." I replied into the phone then disconnected it. I was still caught up in my feelings over Baby, and I think I was more hurt over him taking me off the track than the fight. I needed to figure out a way to get rid of these bitches and fast. Cori thought she was running shit and Blake hoe ass came in and stole my spot. I knew it was only a matter of time before they would replace me because the bitch could sing. So once again, I was going to figure out a way to eliminate that hoe.

19

Mic Check 19

YUNG BABY

"Ma stop tripping, you look fine."

"It's not that, what if she doesn't like me?"

"She's gonna love you. Trust me, my ma dukes love anybody I love."

"Okay." Blake began smoothing down her dress nervously. I grabbed her hand and walked her into the gate where my entire family was. It was the day of our family reunion so the entire yard was packed. Like always, the event was held at my moms crib. Everyone flew in from out of state. I couldn't wait to see my G Moms with her crazy ass.

BLAKE and I entered the gate and the first person I spotted was my uncle Larry. He was talking to two chicks I never seen, and I was sure my cousin Brianna invited them. Brianna was one of my cousins that I also looked out for. She decided to leave her moms and come back to the city and open up a business. Her bougie ass was a real diva.

Her shit was located in the heart of Beverly Hills and everything cost a grip.

"Nephewwww!" uncle Larry spotted me and walked over.

"Sup Unc." we gave each other a hug. I chopped it up with him for a few then walked off because I was anxious as hell to see my granny.

BLAKE and I walked towards the crib and I stopped 50 times to talk to my peeps. I couldn't get to granny fa shit. When we finally walked into the house, I pulled Blake along with me towards the den where I was sure mom was entertaining.

"Son, you gone live a long time. We were just talking about you." my mother said excited to see me.

"Sup ma? Hey aunt Vee, hey Michael." I spoke to everyone while giving my moms a hug.

"Hi baby, what's your name?" Mom asked looking over at Blake.

"I'm Blake." Blake extended her hand.

"Peanut!" my granny shouted calling me by the name she called me as a kid.

"Wanda!" I smiled, running over to her. To everyone else she was grandma, but to her, she was Wanda. She hated when we called her granny or anything that made her feel old. "What's up with you old lady?"

"Hell drinking this weak ass shit yo mom put in my cup." she said looking into her cup of liquor.

"Yo ass don't need to be drinking anyway."

"Boy, I'm grown." she rolled her eyes. I swear my granny thought she was young. "Where my baby?" she said referring to Mani."

"She with her moms. They should be on their way."

"Oh okay. And who dis pretty little thing?"

"That's my girl Blake Bailee."

"Girl? As in girlfriend?" her eyebrows raised. She looked from over the bridge of her glasses like a real creep. I swear my granny was a creep yo.

"Blake, what's your secret baby? Cause this man been a hoe all his life." My granny laughed making everyone else laugh with her.

"Oh mama, leave my baby alone. Blake, don't listen to this lady; she's crazy." my mother jumped in and rescued me. Granny was gone go in on ya boy like she always did. "Blake baby come in the kitchen with me so I can make you and this crazy boy some drinks and food."

"Ma, I don't want no weak shit." I said mimicking granny.

"Oh hush." she said and grabbed Blake by the shoulders. They headed into the room and granny zoomed right in on my ass.

"You know Tris funny looking ass coming." she said making me laughing. She always cracked jokes on Tris. I don't know why, but she really didn't care for her. When I first flew Tris out to granny's, it was her 60th birthday. She bagged on Tris the whole night. By the time we left Tris had the nerve to say "I don't think yo granny like me." I wanted so bad to say *no shit*, but I played it to the left.

"I already know Wanda."

"Aight, I don't want no shit. Now if I gotta get out of this chair it's gone be trouble."

"Wanda, yo faking ass don't need that chair anyway." I laughed so fucking hard.

"It's fa my insurance, mind ya business." she shot then rolled off on me. I was laughing so damn hard I was bent over with tears damn near coming from my eyes. Granny was a straight fool and this was why I couldn't wait to see her. I missed the fuck out of her. I made sure anytime I was in the *A*, I would visit and when I missed her most I'd fly out on the jet. Wanda was my rock, so I made sure to take great care of her. She had a fat crib just like moms and I kept all her shit paid.

I WALKED OUTSIDE SO I could go mingle with the rest of my family. Because I was always so busy, I made sure to put everything off for this weekend. Granny was staying for a week along with my aunt Jackie and Uncle Larry so I was gonna make sure I came back to chill. I walked into the yard and the smell of BBQ filled the air. All my little cousins ran around the yard and my big cousins mingled with each other.

"Baby, let a nigga hold something." I looked down at the voice. I shook my head laughing because Brianna bad ass son Marjay rolled up on me like he was a grown ass man. Nigga was eight years old but the way he talked you would never know it.

Shaking my head I reached into my pocket and peeled off 5 one hundred bills.

"Here bad ass nigga." I handed them to him, and he smiled wide. I know the nigga didn't need it because his mother was rolling in dough; he just had to fuck with me.

"What them grades looking like?"

"Man I got all A and B's." he boasted with the money in the air like he was counting it.

"Boy if you don't quit that fucking lying." Brianna walked up out of nowhere. Marjay looked at her like he wanted her to shut up.

"Ma."

"Don't ma me while you over here lying and shit. This foo got three F's on his last report card. That's why he got on them *Paw Patrol* shoes." she said and I looked down. I bust out into a fit of laughter because sure enough this nigga had em on. Anytime he fucked up in school Bri would make him wear unnamed branded shoes and clothes. She always kept him fresh in red bottoms and Gucci so this was punishment fasho.

"Hey cousin." Bri said and gave me a hug.

Marjay ran off embarrassed but that was cap. He had that 500, so he wasn't worried bout what his moms was talking bout. "Where my little cousin?" she asked and it made me look down to my phone.

I sent Tris a text wondering what took her so long. Because Blake was here, I told her just drop Mani off. She was supposed to have been here already and I was hoping she would have come and left so it wouldn't be no shit. I wasn't really worried because Blake and I were together so Tris would have to understand. The night after we left the restaurant she asked me a million times about Blake, so I ended up admitting Blake was my chic. Well at that time she was still mad at a nigga but I knew she would be mines again. Blake wasn't going nowhere so it was about time the world knew. Which is why I decided to bring her here today. I knew it was only a matter of time the media will blow it up but Mill loved the idea.

20

Mic Check 20

BLAKE BAILEE

I sat in the kitchen for about an hour chilling with Baby's mother. She was so cool and made me feel at home. Now his granny on the other hand, she rolled her ass in here asking me a million questions. A few times I was stuck because she asked me questions about my background. When Ms. Taylor handed me the plates, I was saved by the bell. I excused myself and headed outside to find Baby.

WHEN I GOT outside he was standing in a circle amongst three girls. I walked over to him and handed him his plate. The girls got quiet except one.

"You must be Blake?" one asked and extended her hand. "I'm Brianna, Baby's cousin. This is Carigan and Shayonna.

"Hey." I replied and the girls shook my hand. Their vibe seemed pretty cool and to my surprise they didn't seem thirsty over Baby.

"Thanks ma. She ain't give you..." before he could

finish I pulled his hot sauce from my bag. My hands were full so his mother stuffed it inside my purse.

"My baby." he smiled and took the plate along with the sauce.

"Daddy!" we all turned around and a little girl ran over straight to Baby.

"What's up Mani baby." he replied with a huge grin. I had learned that Mani was his daughter and not his girl-friend. Speaking of, Tris walked up on us and her eyes immediately darted over to me.

"Hey Tris." the girl Brianna hugged her but I didn't say shit. Instead, I began picking from my plate.

"What's up baby daddy?" she looked at Baby.

"Sup Tris." he replied unmoved as he handed his daughter a piece of chicken. I couldn't keep my eyes off Mani because she was so cute and looked just like Baby. This was my first time seeing her in person other than the short glimpse at the restaurant. He had plenty of pictures of her around his home but I had never met her personally.

"Where mama?" Tris asked with a slight eye roll.

"In the house." Baby replied dryly.

Tris walked off towards the house but making sure she hit me with one last look. I knew that as long as she was here shit was gonna be awkward but I ain't pay it any mind. Mani zoomed right in on me and for some reason she began asking me questions. I swear she was like her damn great grandma. However, she was so cute so we indulged in a kiddish conversation. Before I knew it, she was all over me. She called herself teaching me Spanish and I could tell now, she was a handful.

$$$

"BAE, YOU BOUT READY TO ROLL?" Baby asked half drunken. It was almost 1AM, and we spent the entire day drinking and partying with his family.

"Daddy I wanna go too!" Mani shouted running over to her dad. I swear this girl was a live wire because she was still up with energy.

"Daddy got work tomorrow ma."

"But... but... but Blake could watch me." Baby looked at me and I shrugged. "Tell daddy you stay with me Blake pleeease..." she whined and I couldn't turn her down.

"It's okay bae, I'll stay with her."

"Aight go let yo mom know you leaving baby."

"Okay." she ran off into the house. Tris was still here and had been all day. I knew she was only here to watch me but to my surprise she didn't trip. She kept her cool, and I was sure it was because Baby was crazy, and she knew not to test him.

"We bout to get out of here." Brianna walked over. "Nice meeting you Blake. And Baby I'm coming to the show. You're performing right?" she looked over to me. I didn't know what to say, so I looked at Baby.

"Hell yeah. We bout to drop that new track I sent you." he replied.

"Okaaaay, Cinderella." she smirked in my direction. I instantly began blushing.

"We gone rock that bitch." Baby spilled rubbing his hands together.

"Okay, I'll see you guys there." Brianna walked off. Her friends waved goodbye to me and I politely smiled good-bye. They were so cool. The entire day it was pretty much Brianna, myself and her two friends. Baby would always wander off but he made sure to keep checking on me. I

129

couldn't front, I really enjoyed myself. The yard still had a few people in it, but it was pretty much dead. The DJ didn't leave until 2am and I could tell the old heads were gonna hang out all night.

"Where she going?" Tris walked out saying.

"She going to my crib."

"Mmmm." Tris looked at him strangely. "You ain't gone have my baby at your studio while bitches fighting and shit?" she asked sarcastically.

"Man what the fuck you talking about?" Baby replied annoyed. I knew she was talking about Cori and Liv because Cori had called this morning and gave me the rundown.

"You know what the fuck I'm talking bout."

"Mannn, whoever telling you shit, did they tell you I wasn't even there? Tris you know if I was there the shit wouldna went down. Better yet, scratch that, I would have let Cori beat Liv ass no questions asked. But real shit, that ain't yo fucking business. Now where's Mani sweater?" he asked dismissing her. She smacked her lips and walked off. She came back shortly with Mani's jacket and Baby grabbed it from her then motioned for me and Mani to leave.

AS WE DROVE HOME, Mani was in the back seat talking up a storm. Baby drove in silence and I could tell he was contemplating something. I was more than sure it had to do with Tris and it actually bothered me to the point I wanted so bad to ask him. Knowing how Baby was, I knew he needed his space when he was upset.

"What's up Blake, why you keep looking at a nigga?" he asked without looking my way.

"Just wondering what's bothering you."

"Shit, my BM. I swear everything that goes down in my studio this bitch be knowing. Mill nor Bang don't fuck with her period."

"What about Liv?"

"It's possible but real shit they never got along. So I kinda doubt it. Whoever the fuck it is, when I find out they betta hope I don't slice they fucking throat. I don't put her in my business so I don't understand why would they feel the need to."

"You right." I replied then focused my attention ahead. It wasn't my place to speak on his and Tris business, so I remained quiet. By the time we pulled up home, I looked to the back seat and Mani was knocked out. It was late as hell so I knew she was tired. I prayed like hell her ass slept all night because I was good and drunk and I wanted to slide up on something.

Since the first time Baby and I had sex, we had been going at it like crazy. I made a mental note to self to go get some birth control because this nigga refused to use a condom. Crazy part was, he kept them right on the side of the bed in his night stand. The way he had me feeling, I knew if I didn't get protected I would for sure be having a baby, Baby.

21

Mic Check 21

BLAKE BAILEE

The sound of my phone ringing woke me from my sleep. I knew it could only be either Baby or Cori because they were the only two that had my number. Baby had upgraded my phone and changed my number so I would stop receiving texts from Lenox. Two weeks ago he had texted me begging me to come back. He also asked me questions about what did I tell the hospital so I knew then he was scared. I guess he thought that I had told on him but truthfully I wasn't even worried about his ass. After the ass whooping Baby and his crew put on him, I was sure he had learned his lesson. He tried to use the fact that his arm was broken and his ribs were fractured to make me feel sorry for him but the shit didn't work. Replying to him with a fuck you emoji, I guess he got the hint I wasn't fucking with him because he finally gave up.

"HEY BAE." I answered the phone groggily and lifted up so I could take the call.

"Aye ma, turn on the radio to the alarm clock." Baby

spoke eagerly into the phone. I reached over and hit the power button then he informed me to go to Power 106. When I turned to the station, my heart sank instantly.

"You hear it ma?" he asked and I could hear the huge grin on his face.

"Yes, oh my god." I squealed nearly in tears. I listened to my voice on the Ghetto Cinderella track and the more I sang the more I became emotional.

"Dope shit." he said making me smile harder. For Baby this was normal, but because I was on the track he sounded excited. "A nigga proud of you. Now I gotta get you in the booth so you could record an EP. 4 to 6 songs. Then we gon work on a whole album for you."

"I don't know Baby. I don't think I'm ready...."

"Well you gotta get ready Blake Bailee because this only the beginning. My baby finna be a star." he boasted making me smile. "And guess what else?"

"What?"

"We got a show tonight. So be ready about 4PM, so I can take you shopping."

"Oh my god, a show?"

"Hell yeah. We gon perform Cinderella. That's the only song so you got this. Give you a chance to get used to that stage. I'mma see you in a couple hours though."

"Okay." I replied nervously.

"Blake." he called out to me before we disconnected.

"Yes."

"Stop sounding nervous, it's too late for that." he laughed into the phone. Shortly after he blew me a kiss then disconnected the line before I could reply. I dropped the phone on the side of me and laid my head back on the board. I needed to recollect myself right now because a bitch was overwhelmed.

．　．　．

ONCE I GOT MYSELF TOGETHER, I called Cori.

"HEY RAP STAR," she answered and giggled.

"Girllll, I'm not ready for this shit."

"Well you betta get ready because Baby ain't playing. That nigga been making beats and shit for you."

"I know, girl; he talking bout a EP. But check this, I'm performing tonight with him."

"Ahhhh! That's dope as fuck!" Cori excitedly screamed into the phone. I couldn't help but laugh and real shit I needed the laugh right now. "Blake, just like I always told you, on the fucking stage. Ain't no mistakes just like at the club. So bitch what you wearing?"

"Not sure. He said he'll be here to take me shopping."

"Fuck that we bout to go now. And we can get some breakfast."

"Okay, well let me get up and slide something on."

"Okay, his daughter not there right?"

"No he took her home."

"Okay, well be ready, I'll be there in about 20."

"Okay."

I JUMPED up from the bed and began pulling out something to slide on. Deciding to slide on a crop top and some sweats I went to take a quick shower because I knew Cori would be here shortly. Before I got in, I made sure to send Baby a text letting him know I was leaving with Cori, within seconds he replied *okay* and also added *come to the studio after y'all eat*. Oh, lord, I was hoping his ass wasn't trying to make me record because I was still on a high from knowing I'd be performing. I wasn't ready for this shit, but fucking with Baby I had no choice. So just like Cori said, I

134

was gonna try my best to own the crowd. This was a different ball game from stripping because it was easy to seduce men, however, the crowd would consist of all genders and races and I think this is why I was so nervous.

$$$

"I'M HIS GHETTO CINDERELLA, rainy days umbrellas.
Gucci shades when we together,
We pack Ninas and Berettas.
Baby down for whatever, and I'll neva let you goooo
We gone be together and let the whole world knowww."

I SANG into the mic behind Baby as he moved back and forth across the stage rapping. I couldn't help but smile with confidence because the crowd was so in tune with me. Baby had made me come out first and when his part came he ran from behind the stage and the crowd went chaotic. I couldn't believe they were singing along to our song and it had just dropped a few days ago.

"Would you be my ghetto Cinderella?" I was knocked out of my daze by Baby who had just walked up on me. He licked his lips sexy as he looked me in the eyes. I was so caught up being smitten by his boldness I began to blush. The sound of clapping echoed throughout the arena and it pulled my attention from Baby. This was my cue to exit the stage so he could continue to perform. I walked off sexy because I could feel his eyes watching me. By the time I made it to the back, his next track dropped and the crowd went into a frenzy. It was one of his older songs but because it had made the Billboards 100 charts it was a big hit.

"BITCHHH! YOU DID GREAT!" Cori shrieked with excitement.

"I was nervous as fuck." I replied but making sure to keep my eyes on the stage.

"You didn't look like it. Girl, you made for this."

"Awe thank you friend." I gave her a hug and we both laughed. I turned back for the stage and watched my baby do his thang. Letting out a deep sigh, I was relieved it was over. To my surprise I was nervous but I sounded good. I was looking good in a black leather skirt, a Nipsey Hussle crop with a half army jacket that Cori picked out. I wore a pair of YSL heels that I managed to work the stage in. My hair was in a long jet black weave that Cori curled up for me and my makeup was done by Glen Yvonne backstage.

WHEN THE CROWD began to clap, and the room went dark I knew it was time. The only light that lit up the room were from the fans' cell phones. Seconds later, a blue light came on and Nipsey's picture appeared on the screen above. As the tribute began to play the entire BBE came onto the stage.

I'M PROLIFIC, so gifted
   I'm the type that's gon' go get it, no kidding
   Breaking down a Swisher in front of yo' building
   Sitting on the steps feeling no feelings

. . .

NIPSEY'S VOICE filled the air and it was a sad moment. When the song went off, the beat dropped to *Last Time That I Checked*. YG walked out onto the stage and began dance walking. He did this dance while Nipsey's part played. When his part came on he began rapping and by this time the crowd were back on their feet. Just seeing the way the crowd went crazy over him made my soul cringe. It's like I could just feel the love in the air. The city loved YG and Nip so this was a blessing.

THINKING ABOUT MY PERFORMANCE, I began to think of those days that I would lock myself in my room and hold my own concert with the half broken broomstick. What was crazy was, I would always imagine myself performing inside of the Staple Center and here I was. Just the thoughts alone brought tears to my eyes. I was so overwhelmed, I couldn't help it. I had been through so much in 18 short years. It's like I had no one to talk to about it because I was too scared I'll get judged. I told myself over and over to tell Baby the truth about my life but I would always freeze up. No one knew the truth but Lenox and my mother. Not even Courtney knew how I ended up in my situation.

"You good ma?" Cori asked rubbing my back.

"Yes, I'm fine. Just can't believe this shit. It's like it's happening overnight."

"Well believe it because from this day forward, you're a star." we held each other's gaze for a short moment and it was evident Cori saw the transition I saw. Over fucking night, I went from a stripping dancing prostitute to a ghetto Cinderella.

22

Mic Check 22

YUNG BABY

6 months later

In the last six months, Blake and I had been tearing up every city and state from *Chi* to the *A*. It's like it wasn't no more Baby; it was now Baby and Blake Bailee. I couldn't do an interview without them asking about her. Just that fast Blake Bailee now had a name in the industry. She had about 12 songs now that were doing hella good. Right now between the both of us, we had the stations on lock, iTunes charts and the Billboard charts. My phone constantly rang for Blake to do features for some heavy hitters in the industry. The media tried to compare her to Rihanna and it was true. She could sing her ass off and remained sexy at all times. Although I hated how all these niggas were throwing them self at her, I loved the attention she was getting. These punk ass niggas stayed in her DM. Crazy part, they knew she belonged to me, but they didn't give a fuck.

. . .

RING....

THE SOUND of my personal ringing made me look over. I had my business phone powered off because today I didn't wanna be bothered. It was the first day Blake and I were finally able to relax, and I was trying to enjoy this day with no work.

"Yo?"

"Nigga, who the fuck is Linda Bailee?" Mill asked sounding like he had run a marathon.

"Shit I don't know."

"Well nigga it got something to do with Blake. Turn to channel 99." I grabbed the remote from the side of me and turned to the channel. There was an older lady sitting on the sofa, and she wore a crooked wig with a huge smile plastered on her face.

"So how is your relationship with Blake Bailee?"

"Ooh, Blake and I have the best relationship. She's everything a mother could ask for."

Blake, mother? I thought staring at the screen.

"Let me hit you back." I told Mill and began screaming for Blake who was in the restroom. Moments later she came out, but she didn't look at the screen. I looked at her puzzled because many of times I've asked her where was her mother, and she mentioned her mother gave her up for adoption. I nodded my head towards the screen and when she looked up, she frowned. She eased over to the foot of the bed and took a seat. The more she watched the interview the more she frowned upset.

"This bitch is lying!" she screamed out and looked over at me. Tears were pouring from her eyes, but I was still puzzled.

"I thought you didn't know who she was, and she gave you up?"

"I...she... I don't know Baby. The bitch gave me up as a kid." she cried.

"So the bitch doing this because she tryna come up off you?"

"I guess." she wept.

"Come here." I told her and brought her into my embrace. I powered off the TV because I could tell this shit was painful to watch. I began rubbing her back and trying my best to console her. I don't know what this lady motive was, but a nigga was gonna have to holla at her for sure. If it was money she wanted, that was up to Blake. She had her own account where all her money went to from shows and sales. Although she was my girl, she was now an artist so her bread belonged to her.

$$$

"SO HOW SHE DOING?"

"Man she fucked up. The bitch gave her up as a child and now she just pops up out of nowhere doing shit for clout."

"Man, that's fucked up." Mill shook his head.

"So she ain't tryna repair their relationship?"

"I asked her what she wanted to do, and she said fuck her. So I guess not."

"I don't blame her."

"Shit me either." I replied and stood to my feet. A nigga had been in the studio all night so I was ready to roll. I pulled out my phone and sent Blake a text to meet me and when she replied *okay* I grabbed my bag and tossed it over my shoulder.

"What y'all bout to do?"

"Shit hop on the jet. Fly over the ocean and fuck." he began laughing, but I was dead ass. I was about to take my baby on my private jet and bend that ass over. I hadn't seen her since I left her last night.

"Aight foo." Mill and I slapped hands just as Liv was walking through the door. This was another reason I was trying to shake because I was trying to miss her session.

"Hey Baby."

"Sup Liv." I replied without looking at her.

Ever since Cori gave her that ass whooping she had been acting cool. However, when Blake was around the bitch had a death in her eyes. She hated the fuck out of Blake and the feelings were mutual. Blake didn't fuck with her whether it was during shows, the studio, or wherever. Liv still performed a little but lately she had been slacking. Just because Blake was now signed didn't mean we wanted Liv gone. Fans loved Liv and her whole style so she was still a great asset to the BBE. But for some reason I felt her slipping away.

PULLING UP TO THE LOCATION, Blake was already here and waiting. I grabbed my blunt from the ashtray and my bag then climbed out. When she spotted me, I could see the smile on her face as she leaned against her whip to wait for daddy. I swear being around Blake was a breath of fresh air. We never argued, we didn't disagree and her personality always matched mines. I loved how baby girl was always down for whatever I presented.

"Sup stink?" I kissed her and she wrapped her arms around me.

"Where we going?"

"Just flying."

"Oh." she shrugged and grabbed my hand. I led her on to the jet, and we walked to the back to take our seats.

"Turn some music on." I told her as I grabbed a bottle of Ace from the table.

"Girl we bout to fuck and you wanna hear Lil Wayne?" I laughed hard as fuck making her chuckle.

"My bad." she batted her eyes flirtatiously. She changed the music and Aaliyah began singing through the speakers.

NOW THAT WE have come to know each other
I'll never go away, love will always stay here forever
Cause this thing we've got is very rare, yeah
So don't ever go nowhere, no

I HANDED HER HER GLASS, and she took a seat beside me. I lifted my cup in the air for a cheers, and instantly she began blushing.

"What's this to?"

"A rich muthafucking life. Now take that shit off." I sat back and waited for her to peel out of her clothes. She took a sip from her drink and sat it on the table. By this time we were already up in the air so a nigga was ready. Out of all the fucking I've done in my life, I never made love on my jet. This shit was too intimate and I didn't get intimate with bitches. I fucked them and left but Blake, yeah, baby girl deserved this dick on some rich life shit.

I WATCHED Blake as she strutted over to me asshole

142

naked. When she rubbed her fingers through her hair my dick grew so hard my shit was about to burst. She straddled my lap facing me then bent down to kiss me. When she pulled back, she looked me in the eyes, and we held each other's gaze for a short moment.

"I love you Baby." she spoke slightly above a whisper. I looked her further into her eyes, almost to her soul. I knew she loved a nigga but it was something about the way she said it.

"I love you more shorty." I replied and without warning she slightly lifted up and put my dick at her opening. Using the tip to get herself wet, she had already begun to moan. Sliding down on my dick I could feel her walls locking around my shaft. Her pussy was good and warm I was gonna try my best not to nut prematurely. Man Blake had that fire, fire.

"Mmmmm." she moaned into my ear turning me on more. I grabbed her fat ass into my hands and began guiding her up and down. As she began to ride faster, she threw her head back giving me full access to kiss her neck. I began kissing and sucking, but I hoped I didn't give her a hickey.

As I continued to guide her up and down, I could feel her juices running from inside of her.

"This my pussy forever ma." I spoke into her neck. I could tell what I said turned her on because she began going faster and moaning louder.

"Fuck, I love this dick!... Mmmmm Baby, I love it!" she was shouting so loud I knew my pilot heard her but so what. This was my world and my shit.

"Let it out baby." I told her as I began to slam inside of her. I knew she was nutting because she stopped moving and left me to do all the work. I was pounding her shit so hard, the sound of her ass slapping against my thighs made a beat of its own.

"Ohhhhh..." she let out a cry-like moan as her head was trained out the window. When I looked over, we had just flew through the clouds and the sun beamed through the window. Her juices flowed onto my leg and I don't know what it was, either her pussy juice or the scenery, but I could feel my nut shooting up from my sack.

"Fuuuck Blakeeee!" I growled following her nut. I shot every last drop inside of her and even while my shit was going soft I was still pumping. "I'm putting my son up in this pussy." I told her meaning every word. We both had reached our climax and was breathing like we ran a race. When we caught our breath, right on cue we both reached for a drink.

"This is life." she said looking out the window.

"Hell yeah. The view dope, pussy good, what more can a boss ask for."

"I got the dopest nigga in the game, with his dick inside of me, drinking Ace, on a private jet." she smirked making me smile.

"I told you it was your world Blake Bailee."

"I ain't never leaving either. And I'll cut your dick off if you think you leaving me." again she smirked but this time I didn't laugh. *Damn, this girl love me.* I thought watching her as she watched the clouds. I didn't bother to reply because I was on a cloud of my own. Shit the feelings were mutual, so I guess I'll cut her pussy off if she ever thought about leaving me. This shit was till death, and like I said, I was putting a son up in her. Sooner than later.

23

Mic Check 23

BLAKE BAILEE

"I ain't never leaving, nooo no
This shit is to the death of me, I hope he knows
I ain't never felt love like this nooo no
This shit is to the death, that's on my soul."

WITH MY EYES closed I sang into the mic feeling every lyric in my soul. This song had me so emotional I tried my best not to cry. It expressed how I felt right now in my relationship with Baby but for some reason I felt a pain. That pain came from the thought of him ever leaving me or me leaving him. And that shit hurt. I never in my life felt love like this. I didn't have no mother, no father, no one in my corner so to be truthful I didn't know love felt like this. Being with Baby had me on a high and it felt like I was dreaming. This man was heaven sent and I now understood what Keyshia Cole meant.

"That was perfect; now give me one more ad-lib. We don't need much because we don't wanna overcrowd it." Million spoke into the headphones. I nodded my head okay, and the beat came back on. Shortly after, Baby walked into the studio and my palms began to sweat. I was glad I was only doing my ad-libs because I was embarrassed, which was crazy.

BOPPING MY HEAD, I was riding the beat in my mind. I looked over to the chair Baby had just sat in, and he wore this look on his face as if he was angry. This wasn't like him. Normally when I was in the studio he would come in all pumped up and fuck with me behind the glass. I hit him with a smile and I don't know if I was tripping but it looked like he slightly rolled his eyes. My heart began to pound in my chest and when I was done with the last part, I removed the headphones and walked out of the booth.

"Hey Ba..."

"Man, what the fuck is this?" he cut me off with his face frowned up.

"What's what?" I nervously walked over to him. He held his phone up for me to see and when I zoomed into the screen it was a picture of my mugshot. I studied the picture as if I was trying to figure it out. He swept to the side and there was my other mug shot. He didn't even have to swipe a third time for me to know that my third mugshot was from the last time I was arrested. When I looked at the site, it was posted on the messiest sight of all The muthafucking Shade Room. There was nearly 80k likes and the picture had only been posted 34 minutes. I dropped my head because I couldn't stand to face him. I was caught red-handed and now I regretted never confessing.

"Prostitution dawg?!" he shouted demanding me to look at him.

"It was..."

"It was three fucking times. But it really don't matter

my nigga because it happened and you didn't tell me." he jumped to his feet. "Whole time you a fucking hoe." he shook his head. "I'm in love with a fucking hoe!" he kicked the chair over making it crash into the wall.

"Please Baby let me explain." I began to cry hoping he just listened.

"Explain? How the fuck you gon explain this shit Blake? Do you know how fucking embarrassing this is. A nigga parading you around town like a fucking Cinderella whole time really the bitch in the rags." he shot and after that statement my heart shattered. Tears continued to run down my face and when I looked over at Mill I could tell he felt bad for me. I knew right now, I wouldn't be able to talk to him so I began grabbing my belongings to head out. I looked back at him one last time, and he refused to look at me.

"You don't know my past. You don't know what the fuck I've been through. You brought the glass slippers nigga. I didn't ask for them muthafuckas!" I shot and stormed out. I climbed into my car and headed for Lord knows where. I don't know if he wanted me gone or not but if he did, it didn't matter because I had enough money in my account to move on.

AS I DROVE towards Cori house I thought of the song I had just recorded and it made me cry harder. I had no idea who would leak my pictures but for some reason my mother was the first person that came to mind. I guess she figured after the interview I would run into her arms but when I ignored the whole thing, I guess she did this as revenge. My phone was blowing up so much I knew it was my social media blowing up. Right now I couldn't face the media so when I made it to my destination I was gonna deactivate my page. I had a little over 100k followers, so I could imagine what my comments were looking like. Shit I could only imagine what Baby's comments looked like. And I knew it's why he said he was embarrassed.

BY THE TIME I pulled up to Cori's I was so exhausted from crying I just wanted to lay down. I was hoping Bang wasn't here because I really didn't feel like being bothered. I pulled into her driveway and parked my car. When I walked up to the door, she was already there awaiting me with open arms. I fell into her embrace and cried my heart out right there at her front door. I knew it was possible; my short-lived career was over but fuck that career. I knew Baby was done with me and that's what hurt most.

$$$

"IF YOU COULD HAVE SEEN his face you would have died with me. He looked so disgusted with me Cori. I know this nigga gone leave me so I'mma just go get my stuff."

"He's not leaving you. At least talk to him and tell him your story."

"He doesn't wanna hear shit. Nigga ain't give me a chance to say two words. He called me all kinds of hoes, I'm sure he's done."

"Don't give up friend. I'm telling you that man loves you. And after the story you just told me, he's gonna love you more. You've been through some shit. Hell we all have so I'm sure he'll understand."

148

"I can't believe someone would do such a thing. I don't bother nobody."

"Welcome to Hollywood Blake. This the type of shit the media do. They dig up the negative shit. I guess we were so consumed with the fame we never stopped to think about the bad shit happening like this. Just give it some time; it will blow over."

"To keep it real, I'm not worried about the media anymore. I'm more worried about my relationship." I looked off into the sky. I was tired of crying so I didn't let any tears fall. I was the one to blame so I couldn't be mad at anyone. Plenty of times he asked me who was Lenox and that was my opportunity. Instead I would just say my boyfriend.

"This him right here." Cori said looking down at her phone.

"What he say?" I asked eagerly hoping he would say for me to come home and talk. I had powered my phone off when I got here so I don't know if he tried to call me.

"He just asked were you here."

"Let me see." I asked and she handed me her phone. I wanted to type like I was her but when the next message came through I didn't bother.

BABY: *she with you?* 😒
   Me: yes 😩
  Baby: *keep that hoe over there with you.*
I'm going out of town for a few days.

READING the text over and over my heart was in a million pieces. I knew this nigga wasn't going out of town because this was the first time I've heard of this. Just the thought of him possibly laying up with another chick felt like a knife jabbed into my heart. This time I couldn't hold back my tears. I began sobbing as I handed Cori back her phone. When she read his last message she began texting a mile a minute. I knew Cori and she was probably cursing him out.

"Just let him be friend." I told her and laid my head back on the pillow.

"You can stay here as long as you need." she spoke sympathetically.

"I'mma go look for a house in the am. I can't stay with you." I spoke sadly then got lost in my thoughts. The pain I was feeling right now was worse than when Lenox whooped my ass. I didn't deal with this much hurt even when I left his home. No I didn't regret leaving because now I had my own money but I did regret falling in love. A bitch was sick.

24

Mic Check 24

YUNG BABY

I sat inside the VIP at club Tropicana with my team surrounding me and a group of bitches around us. Taking a sip from my drink I walked over to the banister and peered down to the stage. Blake had just took the stage along with Tay who had collabed with her on a track called *Kill Game*. Once the song was done, Tay walked off and the host brought a stool onto the stage. Attaching her mic to the stand, Blake took a seat and began singing into the mic. She held onto the mic with both hands as she held her eyes closed and fell in sync with the music. She was singing her heart out.

The more I listened to the lyrics my heart pained me. I knew the song was about me and I also could tell singing it was making her emotional. The dim lighting and one single purple light shined upon her making her performance tasteful. Looking around the club she continued to sing and suddenly her eyes fell on to mines. We held each other's gaze for a split-second, until I couldn't take it anymore. I walked away from the banister and took my seat. Taking a big gulp from my drink I tried my hardest to drain out her voice. It's like she was doing something to a nigga.

IT'S BEEN NEARLY 2 weeks since I've seen her and I couldn't front, I was missing her like crazy. However, I had to keep my distance so I could figure this shit out. I was beating myself up because we were now musically attached and I fucked up when I mixed pleasure with business. Whenever she had a studio session I made sure to not show up. I would book her shit in the day because I was really a wee hour type nigga. Right now she was staying with Cori but I made sure to check up on her. Although I was missing Blake, I was disgusted with her. She had plenty of time to tell me about this shit, but she didn't. Cold part, I've asked her over and over did she fuck any of them niggas at the club for money, and she would always say no. It's like she had me thinking everything came out her mouth was a lie now.

She also had me rethinking shit that happened in our past. Like the day she was at the restaurant with that old man. Bitch straight up lied talking about that was Lenox father. Then I noticed she wasn't the only one that lived with that nigga. That nigga was her fucking pimp the whole time. Bang told me to give her a chance and hear her out; he also told me bits and pieces of her life that I was sure he had gotten from Cori. After being away from baby girl for so long I made up my mind to hear her out but not tonight because a nigga was feeling good and I didn't want shit to damper my mood. For the first time today, I had a clear mind about the situation and trust me it took the entire two weeks.

. . .

HEARING BLAKE'S VOICE, I didn't realize she had walked into the VIP. I was so in a zone I didn't even realize she was done performing. DJ Mustard's *Pure Water* was now bumping through the speakers and the atmosphere was back to a club scene. I watched Blake as she made her way over to the sofa and took a seat by herself. A part of me wanted to call her over but a nigga pride was too damn big.

"Hey Baby." I heard a voice and looked up. Draylen was standing at the entrance with a huge smile like she was happy to see me. About four days ago we had finally kicked it and I couldn't front baby had some good ass pussy. Nodding for the security to let her inside, I sat back and watched her long legs in a teal mini dress exposing her thick thighs. She strutted over to me with her purse hanging to her side and took a seat beside me.

"Sup ma?" I asked as I brushed my hand down her leg.

"You." she replied flirtatiously.

"What you doing out here?" I asked because she lived up north.

"Came downtown to grab some stuff for the store."

"That's what's up." I was flattered. After talking to Draylen, I learned she owned two businesses. A smoke shop and a clothing store back at home. That shit turned me on more about her because I loved a bitch with a business mind. "You want a drink?" I asked her and grabbed the glass before she could respond. When I handed her the drink we got cozy and began chatting. When I looked up, I could feel Blake burning a hole through me and I swear I forgot her ass was even here. Her face converted into a frown. Just seeing the pain in her eyes sent me into a daze, that I didn't even hear Draylen call out to me.

"Baby!"

"My bad. Isn't that your girl?" she asked noticing me looking in Blake's direction.

"Ex." I replied then turned to face her.

Blake got up from her seat and walked down the flight of stairs. I wanted to get up and run for her but again my pride wouldn't let me. Instead, I got caught up in a conversation with Draylen but the entire time I was thinking bout Blake.

$$$

AFTER ABOUT AN HOUR, I noticed Blake hadn't returned to our section and this shit piqued my interest. I excused myself from Draylen and walked over to the banister to look down. I scanned the crowd of people who were partying hard and enjoying their night. When my eyes landed on Blake she was standing beside Cori and three niggas stood around them. One of the niggas was in her face and the way she was smiling had a nigga pressured. I motioned for Bang to walk over because I don't think he knew Cori was even here.

"I'mma beat her ass." he said and this was the perfect reaction. I told the crew it was time to roll so we all fell out the VIP leaving the women and even Draylen behind. When we got down the stairs I walked right up on Blake and stood in front of her and her male companion.

"Get yo self fucked up here Blake Bailee." I told her then mugged dude.

"What?" she looked at me like I was crazy. "I'm enjoying the single life just like you." she had the nerve to say only adding more fuel to the already lit flame.

"Nah, you on some hoe shit." I shot and I could tell I struck a nerve. She looked at me like I was crazy then stormed out of the club. I looked back at Bang who looked like he was in a heated argument with Cori and told both of them it was time to roll. We all walked out and I went straight for the bus bypassing the bitches that was trying to take pictures and shit.

WHEN I WALKED ON, I headed straight to the back where I knew Blake was. I snatched the curtain back and when I looked into her face her eyes were flooded with a train of tears.

"Don't you ever in your fucking life disrespect me like I'm so hoe ass nigga. I would have been wrong if I snatched yo ass up and embarrassed yo little nigga friend."

"Just leave me the fuck alone." not being able to control my emotions I forcefully dove at her and pinned her down on the bed. She instantly began kicking and swinging for me to get off of her but fuck that, she had me fucked up. I began choking her ass but not hard. Just hard enough for her to feel slight pain.

"If. You. Ever. In. Your. Muthafucking. Life...." I continued choking her until Cori ran inside and snatched me back.

"Bro you trippin right now." she said looking at me like she wanted to square up. Sis had hands, and she was a bold muthafucka but I swear this would be the day I would beat the fuck out of both these bitches. I looked back down to Blake, and she wore the coldest mean mug on her face. Not wanting to submit to her after what I just done, I stormed to the front of the bus. We were already in motion and I couldn't wait to get off this muthafucka. I pulled my phone from my pocket and hit

Draylen to let her know to meet me at the studio so we can roll out.

"Here nigga. Hit this so you can calm down." Bang said walking over to me and handing me a blunt. I took it from his hand letting out a soft sigh then took a pull from it.

"Man this bitch got me hot."

"I know but it ain't worth losing your cool. Blake a good girl that made some fucked up decisions in life. Don't shit on her like the rest of the world my nigga." Bang said and walked towards the back.

Hearing him speak so positive of her told me he saw something dope in her because Bang was a fool. I guess the thought of love with him and Cori was giving him a different outlook on life and love. Since she's been around he been acting different as fuck but more chill. My nigga was finally happy although Cori tested him on a regular.

I PEERED out the window into the night air and I thought about the future I had planned with Blake. I had made plans to put a baby inside of her and maybe in a year or so, I thought of the possibility of marriage. However, I don't know if I would be able to ever get over this shit. It wasn't just the fact that she was selling pussy because every bitch had some hoe in them; it was the principle of the matter; she lied. Not just one lie, but lie after lie. I knew if I forgave her it would take some time but the question was, did I want to forgive her?

25

Mic Check 25

BLAKE BAILEE

Sitting in the back of the bus I cried my eyes as Cori, my knight and shining armor rubbed my back. I swear I don't know what I would do without her. I couldn't believe this nigga had choked me and even had the audacity to say I disrespected him. The way he was cozy with that bitch in VIP the nigga really had his damn nerves. What got me was, she was the same bitch from the show in Oakland which told me that they still been in contact. I hadn't seen the nigga in weeks and I was sure this was who he was spending his time with. They were just too damn cozy for me.

Not being able to take it, I went downstairs and that's when I stopped to talk to the nigga. Cori had just walked up while I was in the midst of the conversation. I learned that his name was Kenneth and boy was he fine. We exchanged numbers and thank god Baby didn't see that part. He was so damn busy with his little bitch that he made room for me to get to know Kenneth. In that hour, I learned he had no kids, no wife, and he was a d-boy from South Central. I swear if this nigga didn't make his mind up I was gonna see what Ken was about. It was time I lived freely because I didn't have the normal childhood. Baby was my first boyfriend even through my whole life. I didn't have a crush when I was younger because I could barely go outside. At school no one liked me because I was less-fortunate thanks to my crack head ass mother.

"5-0." I heard Bang's voice and he sounded rattled. I then heard scattering around the bus so I got up from my seat and headed to the front. Just as I walked up, a White male officer walked onto the bus with his flashlight out.

"Who's in charge of this bus?" he asked flashing his light.

"Me sir." Baby said but didn't move from his seat. He cocked his head to the side like he was unbothered.

"Do you mind if we search the bus?"

"Yes I mind. Fuck you mean."

"Well we smelled marijuana a mile away and this is a no smoking zone." he said like a complete asshole. However, the officer was right. Although marijuana was legal in California, Santa Monica didn't play that shit. You couldn't even smoke a vape cigarette.

"Can I get back-up." the officer spoke into his walkie-talkie and began giving the location. Baby blew out a hard and frustrated sigh. Knowing exactly why, I closed the curtain and quickly ran to his stash where he kept his gun. I pulled it out and slid it into my hand bag.

"Bitch what you doing?" Cori asked in a panic.

"I can't let him go back to jail Cori. He just got out for a gun." I quickly sat back on the bed like nothing happened and just my luck a female officer opened the curtain.

"You ladies have some ID." she said looking between Cori and I.

"Umm...yes..." I said and reached for my purse nervously.

"Don't move. I'll grab it. And where's yours?" she looked at Cori. My heart sank and I knew it was over for me. She grabbed my purse and when she saw how heavy it was, she opened it then looked back at me. I shook my head then dropped it.

"Ma'am, is this yours?" she asked assuming it wasn't mines. Thinking about Baby and his last case I couldn't let him go back to jail for the same thing. I nodded my head *yes*. She told me to stand, and she slapped handcuffs on me. She then escorted me through the bus and at this point it was empty. When I got outside all the fellas were cuffed up against the wall.

"We got a gun off the girl. She had it in her purse, and she says it's hers." the female officer told another officer who had walked up on her. Baby turned around and looked at me.

"Blake." he said my name low as if he was gonna object but I gave him a sure look. I was escorted to the patrol car and tossed into the backseat. Another officer climbed in and before he pulled off I peered out the window to Baby.

"I love you." I mouthed the words and he nodded his head.

As the car drove off, I could still see him shaking his head and the look in his eyes told me he was worried. I laid back in the seat and prepared for whatever was ahead. I knew I would probably have to fight the case, but I was gonna for sure fight it from the streets. As soon as I got a phone call I was gonna call Cori so she can pick up my property and retrieve my credit cards so I could make bail.

$$$

3 HOURS later I was sitting inside the holding cell and I hadn't made one call. I looked around and cell and let out a soft sigh because I was tired, cold and tired of hearing these bitches crying. There were at least six women inside and from looking at the two in the corner I knew they were prostitutes. They wore short dresses, makeup and wigs that hid their identity. They sounded dumb as fuck bragging about their daddy and that shit made me remember when I was dumb and believing Lenox was really like a father figure. After he beat my ass and the shit Courtney was feeding my brain I came to terms that Lenox only loved Lenox.

"BLAKE BAILEE." one of the girls said excited. I smiled and turned my attention on my nails. She and the other chick began to chatter and I knew they were talking about me.

"Girl what you here for?" blue wig asked.

"She won't be here for too long. Baby coming to get his boo." blonde wig said, and they high-fived each other. I laughed to keep from frowning because Baby wasn't fucking with me right now.

"That nigga so fine, girl you lucky." blue wig said.

"Oh my god." I giggled because these chicks had no chill. They continued to talk to me and because I didn't have shit else to do we all indulged in a conversation. I don't know what time it was but I knew it had to be nearly morning because I was booked at 1:06AM and it's been hours since I've been here. I knew now it was over for any calls until later in the morning so I was gonna just stay woke until I could call Cori.

$$$

LATER THAT MORNING, a deputy came to the cell and unlocked it. She called my name and I jumped up from my seat. I knew my bitch would come get me with no questions asked. The deputy escorted me down the hall and when we walked into a room with glass windows and phones I was puzzled. I mean I knew this was the visiting room but why was I here and not being released was the question.

"Number 30." she said and walked out the room locking the door behind herself. I walked down the dirty walkway and when I got to window 30, I stopped to look up.

MY HEART SANK into my shoes as I stared face to face with Baby. His eyes pleaded for me, and he wasn't wearing that same look of disgust he wore last night. Right now he looked stressed out like he lost his best friend and I felt the same way. Lifting up my blue county pants I sat down on the cold steel seat. I pulled the phone down and began wiping it off on my shirt. I put it to my ear and looked back up into his eyes. I didn't say a word because truthfully I didn't know what to say.

"How you doing?"

"I'm good, I guess. Where's Cori?"

"She at the studio. Don't worry bout her right now

Blake. I'mma go bail you out this bitch soon as I leave. I just had to see you." he said still looking me in the eyes. I nodded my head in agreance. We both got silent until I found my speech...

"Look Baby..." I said but he cut me off.

"Honestly Blake, I tripped out ma. I mean you gotta understand how a nigga felt after seeing that shit and you lied."

"I understand and I'm sorry for lying. I have something I wanna tell you and I hope you don't look at me different. It's a long story."

"Shit, we got 30 more minutes." he said seriously. I looked at him and sighed before giving him a brief summary of my life.

"When I was a little girl, my mother was heavy on drugs. She was not only physically abusive, but she was mentally and verbally abusive too. That bitch barely fed me, talked to me, she didn't care about me. Which is how I ended up with Lenox. She traded me for drugs." my voice began to crack. "The minute I got with him he slapped a wig on me and made me sell my body. I went to jail twice and the third time was when I did that two years. After that I got out and for the first time he made me sleep with him. I was 18, so I guess that's all he was waiting on." Tears poured from my eyes and when I looked at Baby, he had a lone tear sliding down his face. Seeing him cry, knowing how gangsta he was, made me cry more but I continued. "When I was released, he didn't want me back on the streets, so he sent me to the club. And that's when I met your rude ass." I smiled to break the ice. When he giggled it made me feel better.

"Damn ma, that's a cold ass story. I'm sorry you had to go through all that shit."

"I am too, until I met you. Baby, you made me feel like

life was worth living. I've never had a love like this before. Shit, I've never had no one love me in my life. That's why I'm so close to Cori because she's the only one that seemed to care. And Courtney, she had my back through it all."

"Courtney, that's the one that lives in the house and let me in?"

"Yep. I owe her my life. Whenever Lenox would put his hands on me she would defend me, and he would beat her ass too. She didn't care. Her only concern was me."

"Yeah, I could tell she loves you." he said and looked off. "So what made you take this?" he asked referring to the gun.

"Yo last situation." I replied because I knew not to say much on the phone. "I love you and I would do it again." I looked up at him and bit into my lip wondering what the hell he was thinking. He had this look on his face I couldn't read. Again we frame froze our gaze not taking our eyes from each other.

"I love you Blake Bailee." he said so sincere that it made me cry again.

"I love you, too, Baby Damone Taylor." he smiled.

"I'm bout to get you out of here. I'mma go to Tris house and grab the cash since it's closer than going all the way home."

"Mm mm, you bet not fuck her either." I smirked making him laugh. "Speaking of, did you fuck the girl from the club?" I just had to ask.

"That bitch ain't nobody ma."

"Did you fuck her?" I asked again and this time I was more serious.

"Yeah. I did but I swear I'll never do that shit again. I was sure I was done with you and I needed to get my mind off you." he replied truthfully and let out a sigh. It hurt me but I wasn't that sick because I expected it, but just the thought of him sharing himself with another woman had me feeling dizzy. "Man I'm bout to get you out of here. We need to talk and fuck. I been missing the fuck out of you Blake."

Before I could respond the deputy walked in and told us time was up for the visit. We both stood up and there was nothing really left to say because we had said enough. His last words were all I wanted to hear. I was ready to leave and wrap myself in his arms. He blew me a kiss and after I blew one back I watched him walk down the walkway until he disappeared. I walked over to the guard and she led me back up to the cell. Although I was still emotional, I felt better getting everything off my chest. I was in a better mood and I was gonna wait patiently for Prince Charming to rescue his Cinderella.

26

Mic Check 26

YUNG BABY

When I walked out the police station, a nigga felt so much better although I was a bit shaken by the shit Blake had finally revealed to me. I wish she would have been told me all this because I wouldn't have put her through torment. These few weeks we were beefing was torture to not only me but her as well. All I could picture was her sitting on that stage singing her heart out about me. Baby girl had a rough ass upbringing and her mother was the one to blame. This explained why she hated her so much and refused to make amends. The shit she told me, made a nigga tear the fuck up. Shit was sad. I haven't cried since my grandfather passed away and even then I remained strong. Right now I was on my way to Tris crib to grab the 35 gees to bail her out. I had about a good hundred over there in cash and since it was closer I decided to just go there.

JUMPING onto the highway I couldn't get Blake off my mind. The moment she was released we were gonna head home and lay up. Right now I didn't even wanna fuck. Well, y'all know damn well I was gone do that but real shit, I just wanted to hold and comfort her. I wanted to hear more about her childhood and up until her adulthood. I swear just listening to the shit about that bitch ass nigga Lenox made me wanna go handle the nigga.

Niggas like him didn't deserve to live. I wasn't the type of nigga to spectate how a man got his bread but when it came to abuse that shit wasn't cool. Not only did Blake's mother taint her, but this nigga added already to a scorned child. *"Damn Blake."* I said hitting my hands on the steering wheel. I shook my head at just the thought. I swear I was gone get this nigga handled on my mama.

Once Blake was free and cleared her mind after a few days, I was gonna have her do an interview. Not only did she need to clear her name, she needed to regain her fan's support. Any woman that heard Blake's story would for sure love her more than before. Keep shit real, I was gonna even have her write a book. *A Hip Hop Love In Hollywood*, I could picture the shit already. Other than the shit she's been through with her mother and Lenox, we had a dope ass story to tell. Our love wasn't premeditated; it was one of those fairytale types of love affairs, some shit unexpected.

WHEN I PULLED up to Tris's crib, I was puzzled to see Olivia's car parked out front. I swear these bitches were weird because they really didn't even like each other. It was only 9AM which told me either she spent the night or was on a dick mission this damn early. Tris thought that I was gone out of town because after the club last night we were supposed to head out to San Francisco for Blake to perform.

. . .

WHEN I STUCK my key in the door, I pushed it open expecting to see Tris and Liv in the front room but it was empty and quiet. I bypassed the living room and headed towards Tris bedroom. As I crossed the threshold to her room, I could hear chuckling and them talking. I stopped to listen because this conversation piqued my interest.

"Girl, that bitch career over." Liv laughed followed by Tris.

"You foul for leaking that shit Liv. Now, you know I can't stand the bitch but yo ass foul."

"Fuck her. Bitch came in and stole my shine. And when I dig up some more dirt I'm leaking that too. Fuck that pussy selling ass hoe." again they both laughed and by this time my blood was boiling. I was ready to run in with my gun out and blow this bitch head open. I swear she was lucky I ain't have my strap on me because I just had left the jail. Just when I decided to head inside, something Liv said stopped me in my tracks.

"You looking sexy as fuck in them yoga pants. Come sit on my face."

My face frowned up as I waited on Tris's response.

"You so gay." Tris said but I could hear her voice more clear which told me she had walked over closer to Liv. Next, the sound of smacking could be heard as if they were exchanging kisses. *These hoes gay.* I thought shaking my head.

"Take this shit off." I heard Liv's voice again and Tris giggled. I had heard enough. I walked into the room right when Tris was pulling her pants down. Tris didn't see me but Liv's eyes shot up to me and bucked widely.

"So how long y'all bitches been fucking?" I asked leaning on the wall. *Who said it had to be a nigga* I thought of

167

Tris's words that she once hit me with. My heart was pumping so fast my intentions was to beat the fuck out of Liv but I was tryna keep my cool. I really didn't give a fuck about them sneaking and geeking; it was what Liv said about Blake that made me feel pressured.

"Baby, it's not..." Tris went to say but I cut her off.

"Oh bitch, it's exactly what it looks like. I hope y'all hoes ain't been with none of this shit while my daughter be here."

"No, Baby...I swear..."

"Kill the bullshit Tris." I leaned up from the wall and cooley walked over to them. Now I know I said I don't hit women but I never said I wouldn't slap the shit out of a bitch.

WHAM!

I BACK HAND that bitch Liv so hard that she flew off the bed and into the dresser hitting her head.

"Baby!" Tris screamed my name.

"Bitch, shut yo nasty ass up before I blow you bitches' head off. No matter what you and I go through bitch we supposed to be better than that. You cross me over this punk ass bitch!" I was so mad spit was flying. It was real shit. Tris was crazy over a nigga, but she wasn't one of those crazy ass baby mamas that made their baby daddy life hell. We had a cool bond and vowed to never cross each other. But nah, this bitch crossed a nigga and for this cunt bitch Olivia Luv. This bitch wasn't shit without BBE. I made this hoe. When they told me they signed her it was up to me after that and I gave the hoe a chance. Well she blew it because that bitch career was over.

"I would never cross you. You know that." Tris was crying her eyes out.

"It's too late for that." I shook my head in disgust. "I ain't got shit to say to you. If it ain't about my daughter bitch don't call me. Don't ask me for shit, and bitch don't even mention my name. I hope you can live off child support." I spat with fire in my eyes. "And as for you bitch." I looked over at Liv who was scared as fuck to get up off the floor. "Your career is over hoe! And on my life bitch I'll kill any nigga that decided to work with you. You might as well take yo little bread and pack up because on my daughter soul bitch whenever I see you, I'mma let my bitches beat yo ass!" I shouted referring to Blake and Cori. I stomped over to the dresser and pulled out the 100k and walked towards the door. Before I walked out, I looked back at both these low life cum bucket bitches.

"You bitches is a disgrace. I don't give a fuck about how y'all feel about Blake, you hoes will never be able to walk in her shoes. On my life you bitches better keep her off the internet, and out y'all mouths. The next time y'all mention her, it's gone be how sexy she looks in this million dollar dress she about to meet me at the altar in." Tris's face flushed with anger hearing me mention the altar. And with that, I walked out of her crib. She didn't have to worry about me anymore because the friendship we had outside of Mani was a wrap. And that's on my fake hand-icap granny.

27

Mic Check 27

BLAKE BAILEE

"Blake Bailee let's go!" a deputy walked over to the cell and unlocked it. I jumped up from my seat anxious and walked out. I made sure to tell blue and blonde bye and hold their heads up. As I walked out, I couldn't help but think of how fast I had made bail. It had only been about an hour since Baby left, but I was happy to be released. The officer walked me over to the counter and began printing out papers. She handed me the papers along with my property bag that held my dress from the club, my heels and my cell phone. They had informed me my purse was being held for evidence because that's where they found the gun but I didn't sweat it.

AFTER RETRIEVING MY PROPERTY, I was escorted to the front where I had to be let out of a locked door. Once the door opened, I walked out, but I was stopped by the female guard.

"Blake Bailee, stay out of trouble. You have a great future ahead of you." she said with a smile.

"Thank you." I smiled back letting her words sink in.

I DIDN'T SEE Baby in the waiting room, so I walked outside in hopes he was there. I ran down the stairs two at a time trying to get away from this place and fast.

"Hello Blake." I turned around to the mention of my name and my eyes shot open when I noticed who it was.

"Lenox, what are you doing here?" I asked puzzled. He walked over to me and reached out to give me a hug. He pulled me into him and whispered into my ear.

"You make a scene, I'mma gonna blow your brains out right here." he said and I could feel the heavy object pressed into my side. My eyes fell onto a gun he held pressed against me. He then pushed my body towards a gray Buick with dark tints. When I reached the car I couldn't see who was inside, and he opened the back door. He pushed me inside and climbed in behind me with the gun still pointed on me.

"Sup hoe." Champagne said with a wicked grin.

"What do y'all want?" I asked as my heart raced.

"You know what I want." Lenox replied with a sinister smile. "You thought you were gone just up and leave me for dead. Bitch I made you. You out here living the good life and shit but nah, you owe me your life."

"Please Lenox, I'll pay you." I told him as tears began to run down my face.

"Oh you gonna pay me for sure. I have a good date for you tonight. He requested your pretty ass personally. 10 thousand for this good pussy." he said and rubbed his hand across my face.

"Please, noooo." I cried harder wishing this shit was a dream.

"Where to Len?" the guy driving turned to ask.

"We can't take her to the house; her little punk ass boyfriend might come looking for her. Take her to Big Sam's house for now." Lenox said and my face frowned. Big Sam was one of his friends that sold drugs. I've been to his home on a couple dates and I hated it each time. It was a damn trap house that was run down and infested with drug addicts.

"How did you know I was here?" I asked wondering was me being arrested all over social media.

"How did I know." he laughed looking up to the front at Champagne. "Who the fuck you think had y'all bus pulled over? You know you a loyal bitch taking his gun case. You fucked up my whole plan. He was the one that was supposed to go to jail so you can come home but nah you just had to be a dumb bitch and claim his gun." he shook his head. Hearing him say he was the one that had sent the police had me shook.

WHEN WE PULLED up to Sam's I hesitated until Lenox slapped me so hard my head shifted. I got out of the car, and he made sure to stay behind me. Champagne climbed out and headed into the house with us and the car pulled off. When we walked in, the smell of drugs clouded the air and the house reeked of old stale beer and feet. There were two crackheads in the kitchen with glass pipes to their mouths and one man sleeping on the couch under an old dirty blanket. Lenox sat my property bag down on the countertop and my eyes fell onto it wishing I could sneak my phone out.

"That bitch smoked all my shit while I was asleep." I heard a very familiar voice. When I looked up, my mother stood there and our eyes locked. She looked just as shocked as me, but she didn't say a word.

"Say hello to your movie star daughter Linda." Lenox said and laughed.

"What this bitch doing here?" she asked with her face frowned. She looked like she had just woken up. Her clothing was dirty and her wig was crooked.

"She's back. I got a few requests for her good pussy ass." he said and again he laughed. My mother's eyes darted down to the gun, and she looked back up to me. Only this time she didn't have the same disgusted look. She looked more puzzled and concerned. Her eyes then shot over to the property bag then back to Lenox.

"Take her to the back. Claudia on a date in the first room." my mother said and headed into the kitchen. Using his gun Lenox escorted me to the back room and told me have a seat on the bed. He then walked over to the window to make sure it was locked and secured. I shook my head because the shit was painted shut as if this room was where they did all their dirt. I looked down to the bed before I took a seat and when I noticed the blood stains on the dirty mattress I chose to sit on the worn down carpet.

"I'll be right outside this door. You can't get out that window so don't try no funny shit. Champagne about to get you dressed for your date so stop all that crying and shit like this shit new to you." he said and with that he walked out of the room.

Yung Baby

"WHAT THE FUCK you mean she's been bonded out?!"

"Sir, exactly what I said. We can't place the bond because she's already been bonded out and released."

"Can you tell me who at least?"

"I can't give you that information." she said and it pissed me off more. I had already text Cori, and she told me it wasn't her.

"Look I'll give you 5 grand if you just give me a name." I begged. She looked at me then to the screen. I pulled out the money and secretly counted the five grand. I slid it to her on the low, and she took it with no hesitation. She then grabbed a pen and a piece of paper and wrote down the name. When she handed it to me, I got up from the seat and headed out. I read the name on the paper and the name read Jessica Jones. The name didn't ring any bells and Blake didn't have family, so I was curious.

ME: *A do you know Jessica Jones?*

Cori: *Yeah, that's Champagne. She lives with Blake and she dances at the club.*

Me: *aight*

I SAID and drove towards the house where Blake used to live.

WHEN I PULLED up I pulled my strap from the stash just in case I had to shoot this nigga Lenox. Today I wasn't playing with this nigga and he was gonna be a dead man if he pulled some bullshit. I walked up to the door and I began knocking like I was the police.

"Courtney?" I asked when the door opened. When I heard the locks pop I knew it was her. She let me in and told me to be quiet.

"Where Blake?"

"She hasn't been here." she whispered.

"Aight so where that bitch Champagne because her name on Blake bail sheet."

"Champagne?" she frowned. "She's with Lenox." she said and looked at me. "Oh my god Baby." she said worried thinking the same thing I was thinking.

"Look if they come back with her call me." I said and gave her my number. She put it into her phone and gave me a worried ass look.

"This morning I heard Lenox talking to someone on the phone. He was telling them that he had called the police on your tour bus. After that I couldn't really hear the rest because he went into his restroom."

"So that bitch ass nigga the one that called?" I tugged at my chin. I knew she wasn't lying because how would she know my bus got pulled over. "Look Courtney, Blake loves the fuck out of you and everything you've done for her I appreciate it. Walk me to the car." I told her and we stepped out the door. When I got into my whip I tossed her the Gucci bag with the bail money in it. She looked at me like I was playing but I wasn't. I really appreciated this chick.

"That nigga Lenox a dead man, so I advise you to go pack yo shit and leave this bitch. Don't even worry about waiting for him to come because I'mma be watching this muthafucka."

"Okay. And thank you so much Baby." she said with tears in her eyes.

"Thank you ma." I told her and cranked my engine. She walked into the house and I pulled off for my crib. I was about to change my clothes and get in gangsta mode.

AS I DROVE towards my crib my phone began to ring.

When I saw it was a facetime from Blake my heart fell into my lap and I quickly answered it. When the face appeared on the screen I frowned wondering how the fuck she got a hold to Blake phone.

"Baby it's Linda Blake's mother." she said out of breath. I could tell she was outside, and she was walking up the streets.

"How the fuck you get her phone?"

"Look, please I know you're probably upset with me but Blake in trouble. Lenox got her over at Sam's. I saw... I saw...saw a gun. I think he's gonna kill her." she stuttered as she smacked her teeth like the strung out drug addict she was.

"How I know this ain't a setup?" I looked her in the eyes.

"Trust me. I snuck her phone from her jail bag. I acted like I was going to the store but I came to call you." she replied and I don't know why, but something in her eyes told me she was telling the truth.

"Where's the house at?"

"It's on 32nd and Trinity. Third pink house from the corner."

"Aight look. Don't go back there. Text me where you are and I'mma send you an Uber."

"Okay, okay." she replied anxiously. I disconnected the phone and let out a deep sigh. The call was so intense I had pulled over on the side of the road. I gathered myself then sent Mill and Bang a group text. I quickly explained to them what was going on and told them to meet me at the location Linda had given me. Before I pulled off, I said a slight prayer to myself asking Fod to protect Blake. I also asked for his forgiveness because just like I said before, Lenox was a dead guy.

28

Mic Check 28

BLAKE BAILEE

The sound of the door opening made my heart cringe. I looked up and it was Champagne, so I knew what this meant. She had a duffle bag in her hand along with a makeup case. She walked completely into the room and didn't say a word to me. Instead, she pulled a pair of clean sheets from the bag and began making the bed. After she tossed the dress and shoes onto the bed she pulled the makeup box up and looked at me with so much attitude.

"Why do you hate me so much?" I asked her wanting to know what did I do to deserve the shit she had put me through for years. She looked at me like I had shit on me then folded her arms over the other.

"You know why I hate you? Because yo young ass came into my world and basically took my shit. Lenox was mine, and we were supposed to be a family. But nah that nigga fell in love with you and basically said fuck me."

"Champagne, Lenox don't give a fuck about you or me. Can't you see he's using us."

"He ain't using me." she smacked her lips.

"Yes he is. Please if you help me get out of here I'll give

you a million dollars and you can go on about your life." she looked at me and I could tell she contemplated my offer. Well, at least I thought she did. Again she smacked her lips and looked at me.

"Bitch, I ain't never leaving my daddy." she replied like the shit was cute. "Now come on and get this shit over with because your date on his way." I shook my head and took a seat on the bed. She began applying my makeup, and I wanted so bad to beat her ass and make a dash for it but I knew Lenox was on the other side waiting to shoot my ass. Every so often he came in to check on me so that told me he wasn't leaving.

Once we were done I put on the dress and I couldn't stop the tears that fell from my eyes. I was praying Champagne would take me up on my offer, but she wouldn't budge. She sat here like everything she was doing was okay, and I could tell she was getting a kick out of the shit. Once I was completely dressed Lenox burst into the room.

"They're here." he said and sat a plate on the dresser with pure white cocaine on it. I looked at the plate puzzled wondering what the hell it was for. Knowing how most of the tricks used coke I was sure it was for them and especially because this was a crack house.

"What's that for?" although I knew I still had to ask.

"It's for our guest. The more they get high the more money they spend." he replied like he just struck gold.

They? I thought wondering what did he mean. Shortly after, two White men walked in and my heart dropped. One looked at me with so much lust in his eyes and the other zoomed in to the plate of coke.

"Thank you, Lenox. We're about to have fun with her." the man said that was lusting over me. Lenox smiled proudly as he looked me from head to toe.

"Noooo." I said but I knew I couldn't cry. Lenox would have killed my ass right here.

"Have fun with her. Y'all need anymore get high I'm in the front room." he smiled and closed the door. The guy began undressing while the other sounded like he was sniffing up the entire plate.

"You're a pretty one. I requested you personally my dear." he eyed me licking his lips.

By this time he was asshole naked and his little pink dick stood at attention. When he walked over to me, he roughly pushed me onto the bed and positioned himself on top of me. I knew I couldn't fight this, so I laid there numb. My life flashed before my eyes and at this very moment I wanted so bad to just die right here. Faintly looking over I could see the other man stroking himself, and he was now naked as well. I couldn't hold back anymore. Tears fell from my eyes as the man entered me roughly. For some reason I felt faint, then suddenly the sound of gunshots echoed through the home. The man on top of me stopped and the other guy ran to the door and opened it.

POP!

HIS BODY HIT the ground in an instant. I watched his body in awe as blood seeped from his head. Three masked men appeared in the doorway and I knew them figures from anywhere.

"Baby." I cried out and he ran to my side. The man on top of me jumped up in a panic and...

POP! Pop! Pop!

.   .   .

BANG SENT three shots into his body, and he fell into the broken closet door. I jumped up and ran into his arms. I was crying so hard I couldn't do shit but hold Baby tight.

"We gotta go ma." he said and pried my hands from around his neck. When we got into the front room, it looked like a massacre. The first body I stepped over was Champagne. Next, Lenox was laying on his face with bullets rippled through his back and one to his head. As we walked further throughout the home Sam was dead slumped over at the kitchen table. I quickly swooped up my property bag, and we ran out the home full speed. When we reached the truck I climbed into the back with Baby while Bang and Mill rode in the front. I laid my head into Baby's chest and I couldn't stop crying. The entire car was quiet except for the sounds of my weeps. Baby rubbed my hair and every so often he kissed the top of my head. Right now I didn't know how to feel. All this shit had happened so fast I was delirious.

NEARLY AN HOUR LATER, we pulled up to the studio but I wanted to go home. All I wanted to do was relax in the jacuzzi and go to sleep. I've had about enough these last two days. Enough to send someone to a mental therapy session.

"Get out ma. We not staying long." Baby said and lifted from the seat. He opened his door to climb out then held the door open for me. When I got out, he grabbed my hand, and we headed inside the studio. When we walked in...

"Blake!" Courtney jumped up from her seat and ran into my arms.

"Oh my god Courtney." I was so happy to see her, of course I started crying.

"I'm so glad you're okay." she said making me look back at Baby. He hit me with a smile then nodded his head for me to look forward. When I did, my heart dropped.

"Mom?" I asked confused. I looked back to Baby, and he wore a look of forgiveness. And this told me exactly what was going on. My mother was the one that had told him where I was. I was wondering what happened to my cell phone but I assumed Lenox had taken it. Right on cue, she walked over to me and reached her arm out. I looked down at her hand and sure enough she held my iPhone. Again I looked back at Baby and it's like I began to feel dizzy. I looked back to my mother and I really didn't know how to feel at this point. I didn't know whether to hate her or run over to hug her. Talk about tears, I don't think I've ever in my life entire life cried so hard.

"I'm so sorry Blake." were my mother's last words before I fell to the ground and sobbed uncontrollably.

Epilogue

"So Blake Bailee, we're happy you came to share your story. Girl, you got me over here crying and stuff. So how are you and your mother's relationship now?"

"We're working on it. I mean, after she broke down her life story and the things her father had done to her it made me understand. However, it's hard to forgive but I'm trying." I replied and looked at my mother who sat front row of the show. He hit me with a faint smile and a head nod.

"That's good. Well let's get into the rumors that's circulating."

"Oh boy."

"Yes, we hear there's a possible bun in the oven."

"Yes. I'm three months." I smiled proudly.

"Well congratulations."

"Thank you."

"Well ladies and gentlemen, let's bring to the stage Yung Baby."

. . .

THE CROWD BEGAN to clap as Baby walked onto the stage. He took a seat beside me then reached over to kiss me.

"YOU GUYS ARE SO CUTE. Yung Baby, congratulations on the baby."

"Good looking." he replied cooley.

"Do we hear any wedding bells coming?" before he answered he began chuckling.

"Yes, of course. June 22nd. y'all catch the million dollar wedding on BET."

"Well congratulations as well. Y'all be sure to check that out. So are there any up and coming projects you're working on?"

"Hell yeah. BBE doing something different. We focused on Blake's life story that's gonna air on Lifetime. She's also working on a book so be on the lookout for that. As far as the label we just signed another female artist by the name of Meeah Kelly." he said and smiled.

Meeah was released from prison and contacted me through Instagram. I was so happy to hear from her. When I brought her to the studio she sang for Mill, and he wasted no time signing her. Everyone from BBE welcomed her with open arms. Upon receiving her sign-on bonus she used the money to move into her place. Her and Mill could lie all they wanted to, but they were in love. At this point, my life was going great. Me and my mother were trying to repair our relationship but it took time. She was currently clean and Baby gave her an account with a few hundred grand inside. He also copped her a condo out in Downtown LA.

Between having my mother in my life, Cori, Meeah and Courtney I had a family of my own. Not to mention the bundle of joy I was carrying. I couldn't wait until I had my baby. I knew it would slow down my career for a few months but with the book and movie I wasn't gonna be hurting.

"WELL, thanks for coming. Blake, thank you for sharing your story with us. We send our love and blessings and, once again, congratulations. Well, that's it for the night. We hope you guys enjoyed the show. Same place, same time, catch us tomorrow here on the Kelly Irvin show."

THE END!

VISIT My Website
   http://authorbarbiescott.com/?v=7516fd43adaa
   Barbie Scott Book Trap
   https://www.facebook.com/
groups/1624522544463985/
   Like My Page On Facebook
   https://www.facebook.com/AuthorBarbieScott/?
modal=composer
   Instagram:
   https://www.instagram.com/authorbarbiescot

Subscribe

Text Shan to 22828 to stay up to date with new releases, sneak peeks, contest, and more....

Submissions

To submit your manuscript to Shan Presents, please send
the first three chapters and synopsis to
submissions@shanpresents.com

CPSIA information can be obtained
at www.ICGtesting.com
Printed in the USA
LVHW041411300919
632704LV00002B/331/P